Wedding Wings

and other
Short Stories in support of the

British Deaf Association

Alison Lingwood

Contents

Foreword

We all think from time to time that life is hard. Imagine all those regular hardships and inconveniences being compounded by deafness.

Things that most of us take for granted, like learning to drive – imagine not being able to hear the instructions and guidance you are being given in lessons and the test. Imagine being stopped by the police, but not understanding what they are trying to say; imagine wanting to discuss issues with your local parliamentary candidate, only to have them say, 'Oh it's okay. I'll just go next door,' when you tell them you are deaf. These are just a few of the everyday struggles for someone with impaired hearing.

Discounting professionals working in the field, estimates suggest that there are over 150,000 UK users of British Sign Language, and that over 87,000 of these are themselves deaf. Others use BSL perhaps because a member of their family is deaf.

There are benefits too for people who, though they may be able to hear, are non-verbal. Deafness or the inability to speak may be part of a bigger problem. Imagine not being able to tell anybody that you need the toilet, or that you are thirsty or hungry. BSL opens up an alternative means of communication for those people too.

It is my belief that all children should learn BSL as a matter of routine, right from nursery age. They absorb nursery rhymes and songs, and even though these may subsequently be partially forgotten, they would come back in later life if needed.

Many people lose the clarity of their hearing to some degree as they get older and would benefit from this as a supplementary way of communicating.

MP Rosie Cooper tabled a Private Members Bill in June 2021 to have BSL recognised as an official language. This Bill passed unopposed through both houses of parliament in 2022.

Is it a start? Yes, of course but it doesn't go nearly far enough.

All proceeds from my three volumes of short stories, *The Hairdryer died Today, Mission Accomplished!* and *Wedding Wings* are donated to the British Deaf Association, to further their work into promotion, education and information about BSL and other ways to support the deaf community. I hope that you will enjoy the stories and spread the word to your family and friends.

To find out more about the work of the British Deaf Association contact bda@bda.org.uk or 07795 410724

Wedding Wings

A wedding is always a special and exciting occasion. Can you imagine then, the excitement at what may have been the greatest wedding of all? That between the most powerful of gods, Zeus, Greek god of thunder and lightning, and his sister Hera, the goddess of women, marriage and childbirth.

It was a beautiful day, calm and still with a few fluffy white clouds floating lazily high in the atmosphere. This was a double wedding, with Hera's daughter also to be married at the same ceremony. The daughter's part is incidental to this story, except that it meant the ceremony was an even grander and more lavish affair.

Zeus and Hera asked their wedding guests to bring the best, tastiest, most wonderful food they could produce to form the wedding feast. Zeus himself would judge which food was the best and would grant the producer permission to make a request of him, any request at all.

On the wedding day a vast array of succulent and delicious-smelling food was set in front of Zeus and his bride, and they sampled all of it under the careful watch of the producers, until only one tiny vessel remained untasted.

'Ah,' boomed the god, holding it aloft, 'by the colour of this I think it is pine resin.' All the guests applauded. Pine resin was a highly prized commodity in Ancient Greece, used then and now to convert wine into retsina.

But as Zeus tipped the jar he could see that this was different. It was more golden in colour, more viscous and it had a wonderful sweet smell, which totally captivated him and his bride.

He dipped in his finger and took a taste. 'This is by far the best food,' he declared. 'Who produced it? And what is it called?'

A tiny, fat, hairy creature flew in front of his face, humming annoyingly. 'I am Melissa the bee, and I produced it. It is called *honey.*'

Zeus found the little fat insect buzzing around in front of him very irritating, but the honey was sweet and delicious.

'Thank you Melissa.' Then he turned and shouted to the assembled company, 'Honey for everyone!'

The bee buzzed angrily, 'Oh but that cannot be.'

Immediately the innocent looking clouds became more ominous. Their colour changed from white to slate grey as they grouped together and leaned lower to the ground to hear what was said. When Zeus was displeased they could be called upon at a moment's notice, and were in constant readiness.

The little bee was oblivious and kept talking: 'There is only this tiny amount. You see the honey is made of nectar, gift of the flowers. Each flower has only a tiny amount of nectar to give and I have to fly miles to collect it. Being so tiny I can only carry a very small amount at a time, so I have to return to my nest many times a day. Sometimes the rain soaks my wings and I'm unable to fly at all. It takes weeks to collect a reasonable amount. Then and only then can I begin the job of turning the nectar into honey.'

As the breeze grew into a stronger wind, the grey clouds began to gather into larger and larger groups. Zeus was growing bored, 'Yes, yes. Get on with it, what are you saying?'

'Sometimes the flowers close their petals, or have already been visited and I can collect no nectar at all.'

Zeus heaved a sigh and the earth trembled; his patience was known to be short, 'More problems? And what do you expect me to do about it?'

'You promised that the producer of the best food could make a request of you. I would request a weapon, both painful and fatal. Snakes and scorpions have deadly weapons, yet they have produced no food at all for your wedding feast. Surely the honey is worth meeting my request? You did promise!'

Zeus laughed until the earth shook. 'You want a painful and fatal weapon, like snakes and scorpions? A tiny little thing like you, droning on endlessly about your problems? I don't think so.'

'But you promised,' Melissa persisted, fluttering her wings in front of his eyes, until he had had enough of her whining buzz. The darkening sky rumbled ominously, a sure portent of thunder to come.

The god of thunder was getting angry.

'I promised,' he shouted, 'that you could ask; not that I would grant any stupid wish you came up with. Will a painful and fatal weapon stop the rain soaking you? Will it stop the flowers from closing their petals; or perhaps it will move them nearer to your nest, so you won't have to fly so far?'

He laughed and the wedding guests joined in nervously as the clouds continued to gather and listen.

Melissa had one last try; she held up the jar containing the honey, 'No, but that's not the worst of it. It took me a month to collect enough nectar to make this tiny amount of honey, and yet a visit to my nest from a bear or from a weasel can steal that quantity in seconds. With a painful and fatal weapon the message would soon get around that to steal from my nest would result in certain death. Then I would have more honey to offer to the gods; to offer to you.'

She waited expectantly while Zeus deliberated. She hummed backwards and forwards in front of his eyes, until he batted her away. At length the ominous rumblings in the sky subsided and the sun peeped nervously through the clouds. Immediately Melissa began to feel the growth of a sting protruding behind her and she turned to admire it. The sting had a sharp barb at its tip.

'That is your weapon, Melissa. The price you pay for irritating me,' Zeus bellowed at her, 'is that if ever you use your sting, it will indeed prove both very painful and fatal. It will be very painful for your victim. However, it will be fatal for you. The barb will remain attached and will disembowel you as you try to fly away.'

Melissa cried out in protest, but was stopped

by a roar from the god, 'But,' he said, 'the honey is undoubtedly delicious, truly nectar of the gods, and to help you make more of it I will send many thousands of bees to assist you. They will join in the foraging, and in the making of honey and in maintaining whole colonies for the future. And you, Melissa, as annoying as you are, will be the queen ruling over them all.'

Hymenoptera, the order of classification given to insects translates as Wedding Wings. Mele remains the Greek word for honey. It is believed to give us, amongst others, the words melt, mellifluous and caramel.

The Terpsichorean Art

The Terpsichorean Art: it just means dancing but it sounds posh doesn't it? Charlotte's father Victor always called it that, just as he refused to call her Charlie, the shortened form of her name that she preferred. He fancied himself as an alpha male and came across as quite pompous, but he nevertheless loved his little girl dearly. He had been devastated when he lost his wife Ruth to illness. Since Mama's death there were now just the two of them and Papa had indulged Charlie. When she fell in love with ballet, like so many little girls do, he would chauffeur her to lessons every weekend in the Quebec suburb where they lived.

Again, in common with many girls, as she grew older the enthusiasm for ballet waned, but Charlie continued to love the terpsichorean art, her focus now turned to Latin American and particularly to ballroom dancing. Victor was very proud of his little Princess's achievements, displaying the cups and medals she won around the kitchen in their Canadian home and accompanying her whenever he could to various competitions.

This particular weekend was special. It was the last competition which Charlie would be young enough to enter as a junior. After her birthday next week she would be competing against the adults, a proposition both daunting and exciting. Her current partner Oscar would not be able to make that transition alongside her. He was a tall lad, but two years younger than Charlie, and so would not qualify. She would need to find a new dance partner, and she was hoping that she might find someone this weekend.

As usual Papa had accompanied her to the hotel where they would stay for the duration of the event. It was just over a five-hour drive south from their Quebec suburb, into New Hampshire. He had checked out the hotel beforehand and found that it incorporated its own golf course, so with his clubs loaded into the back of the car, they had set off to do what they both enjoyed best.

Disaster struck during one of the practice dances. Charlotte had been thrown round the dance floor during a particularly energetic tango. Trying to show off, her partner had turned awkwardly and wrenched his ankle. Having dulled the pain with a small tot of whisky from the bar whilst an anxious Charlotte sat and looked on, he was swept up by ambulance and taken off to the local hospital. One of the paramedics, a very agreeable young man who told her his name was Mike, insisted that she sit down and have a warm drink, 'for the shock' he said. Of course time would tell that he found Charlie very attractive and was looking for a way to get to know her. He asked whether he could call back once he was off duty and let her know the diagnosis on Oscar's ankle. Meanwhile Charlotte sat and watched the other dancers practising. Occasionally someone took pity on her and gave her a spin around the floor, but it looked like her last competition as a junior was a wash-out.

When Victor returned, flushed with success, from the golf course, he was saddened to learn about his daughter's problems. Charlie had just finished telling her tale when the young paramedic joined them, looking even more handsome now that he had changed out of his uniform.

'Your dance partner's had an X-ray on the ankle,' he told them, 'It's badly sprained I'm afraid, but at least there's nothing broken. He's got to rest it though, I'm afraid he won't be dancing this weekend.'

'Do you play golf, young man?' Papa wanted to know.

'I do, sir. I'm very keen.' He turned to Charlie, and grabbed his chance, 'I also love to dance. I'm not good enough to enter competitions, but if you fancy taking the risk of a spin round the floor, just for fun?' He turned to Victor expectantly, 'and if your father doesn't object …' Victor nodded his approval and Mike held out his hand to her as the band struck up a foxtrot.

It was the start of a wonderful friendship that grew into love, with the couple eventually marrying in her home town. They lived though in New Hampshire. Mike said that no true Yankee could ever really leave the homeland, and it was far enough, but not too far away from Victor, who was very taken up with golf these days. The two men would sometimes seek out suitable accommodation near to where Charlie was competing, spending the days on the links and the evenings cheering her on in the ballroom. Charlie had a new competition partner, and dancing now took her, and Mike who accompanied her when possible, all over the world. She was fortunate in becoming very friendly too with a South African dancer called Hayiya, a gentle lady who showed her the ropes.

It was hard work, and not as glamourous as many people believed. The travelling was arduous; maybe they would only have a day or two in one place, before moving on to the other side of the continent. Charlie had seen dancing as her chance to visit the capitals of the world, and indeed she competed in South America, in Lima, Santiago then Brasilia; then the following weekend she had a competition in New York.

It wasn't always smart cities though where opportunities for dancing arose. From New York she travelled to the West Coast to the Sierra Wilderness of Yosemite to perform at a private party, and one weekend she jetted off to India, with competitions in New Delhi, Kerala and down to the Ganges Delta, where the local dances and costumes took her breath away. She took the opportunities where she could. Whenever possible Mike continued to travel with her, and Hayiya remained a constant friend and support.

Charlie reached the top of her profession, as the competitions gained in prominence on western television and the Latin dances became more popular. She liked the Latin American dances, but her real love remained ballroom. She became known the world over; sought after for television and stage shows, and the offers of work flooded in more quickly than she could deal with them. Mike gave up his full time job to become her manager, fitting in bank work for the ambulance service when they weren't travelling.

On a trip to London the young couple took the opportunity to visit Shakespeare's Globe Theatre, something Mike had read about and always wanted to do. The play being performed on Charlie's only available evening was Romeo and Juliet, but they had not long taken their seats when she began to feel unwell. It was cold for June, and she wondered if she was just very chilled, but it seemed to be more serious than that, and by the time the play was drawing to a close, she was feeling very sick. She barely heard the tumultuous applause and cries of 'Bravo, Well Done, Encore,' echo around the theatre, as she dashed out of the auditorium and only just reached the ladies' rest room in time.

Back home a visit to her doctor confirmed that she and Mike could expect an addition to their family. The first thing they did was to telephone her Papa back in Canada. Mike spoke to him first, 'We have some lovely news for you, Victor. There is to be another generation of dancers, and perhaps golfers too. We are expecting a baby in late November.' He handed the phone over to Charlie, who had let him talk first because she knew she would cry, she was so overcome with happiness.

On the first day of December Charlie gave birth to a little girl who weighed in at seven pounds. On the phone again to Victor, they gave him the details. He would be joining them to meet his granddaughter in just a few hours. Down the phone Mike heard him working out the weight, 'You Yanks with your old fashioned measurements; seven pounds, that's, let me see - one kilo is 2.2 pounds, so she weighs three point three kilos, that's a good weight. I'm so looking forward to meeting her. What are you going to call her?'

Charlie proudly told him that the baby's name would be Ruth Hayiya; Ruth after Charlie's late Mama, and Hayiya, after the lovely African lady who had taken Charlie under her wing and been a good friend for so many years. She had told Charlie when they first met that her name was a Zulu word that meant *Dancing for Joy*.

For Charlie and Mike's firstborn it seemed appropriate.

* There is more to this story than meets the eye. Have you spotted the hidden thread running through it? You will find the answer after the acknowledgements at the end of the book.

A Fine Romance

The book had come to the end of its natural life, and quite a full life it had enjoyed. Bought new in Birmingham, it had been passed round a group of friends and eventually donated to a charity shop. It had been spotted as an ideal present for the book club Secret Santa. Each gift was to be fairly modest, and books, of course, were a favourite with them all.

Anne, the recipient was delighted. She read it and loved the story, earmarking it to take to her friend in Manchester when they next met up. At the next meeting the friend returned it to Anne, and she put it in the collection to go to the local hospital for a top-up to their library trolley.

A woman in the hospital was partway through reading the now tatty book, when she was discharged. The library lady said that of course she must take the book home with her to finish. She had read it herself, loving everything to do with life north of the Arctic Circle, and it was getting a bit too damaged now, with its broken spine, to be suitable for lending out.

And so the book ended up at this lady's home. Her young daughter Kirsten helped to look after her as she convalesced, and they spent time after school listening to the radio together. After a couple of weeks, her mother having sufficiently recovered, Kirsten asked whether they could please go to the book place on the big industrial estate. She wanted to take the tatty book with her.

When they arrived she took her mother by the hand, and led her into the small reception area, where a lady was seated behind a desk.

'How can I help?' she asked with a smile.

'I heard a man on the radio saying that you are saving and squashing books. I've got one here you can have, that my mum and her friends have finished with. Mummy says it's too tatty to give to the charity shop. The pages are coming loose, look!'

The receptionist of the publishing house had been about to go on her lunch break, but the earnest little girl with her mother standing behind her, one hand protectively on her shoulder, made her pause.

'I'm sorry,' the girl's mother said, 'this probably isn't what the radio article meant at all, but Kirsten heard it and remembered some of what was said. She was quite insistent that we at least come and ask.'

'No, I think it's unwanted books from the factory here that are being squashed,' she looked at the earnest face of the little girl, clutching her grubby paperback. 'But I'm sure it will be fine, just give me a minute.'

She turned to the phone, 'Mr Marshall? I have a young lady here who has brought a damaged book to add to our reject pile. I said I thought you would be pleased, is that okay?'

She put down the phone, 'Mr Marshall will be right with you Kirsten, if you and your mummy would like to sit there a moment.'

Within minutes a large man had joined them, and looked from mother to daughter, 'Now ladies,' he said, 'I understand that you have an important book for us.'

'I don't know if it's important,' Kirsten seemed less sure now, 'but if you want damaged ones, look,' and she demonstrated the broken spine and loose pages.'

'Oh yes. We have lots of books here, but I'm sure we can make room for one more. That will be ideal. Would you ladies like to come through and see what we are doing with the books?'

He led them into the production area, where two people with jackets labelled "Quality Control" were sorting through large racks of books.

'There are a number of things that can go wrong with books when they are being made,' he explained, picking up one of the volumes, 'This one for instance has gone a bit askew during the printing process and the words aren't straight.'

Kirsten looked at it and laughed, 'some of them have fallen off the edge of the page. Nobody can read that.'

He smiled, 'Exactly!' and replaced the book, taking up another, 'This one looks okay, until you open it.'

He demonstrated and Kirsten laughed again, 'The cover's upside down.' She pointed to another pile, 'What's wrong with those?'

'Flicking through them, they look fine. The words are straight, and the cover is the right way round,' Mr Marshall paused for effect, 'but find page number ninety two.'

Kirsten flicked through the book and said, 'Oh, but after page ninety two it goes straight to page hundred and fifteen.'

'Hmm,' Mr Marshall nodded agreement, 'A problem in the binding department. We don't just bind one book at once, we do a batch all at the same time.' Occasionally, a group of pages get put out of order, so that those books either repeat a load of pages, or miss them out altogether.'

'I'd be cross if my book did that.'

'So would I,' he said, 'that's why we have people working here to check the quality.'

He pointed to another pile, 'Sometimes the books just aren't popular. People don't fancy reading them and so the shops don't buy all the ones we have printed. There's nothing wrong with this pile, except that nobody wants them.'

'What happens to them all, the damaged ones and those that nobody wants?' Kirsten was interested to know.

Mr Marshall pointed to two large skips, into which the Quality Controllers were tipping pile after pile of books. 'These are going to a huge recycling plant down in South Wales. They will shred them all, then pulp them up with water to make them soft and soggy enough to use.'

'What for?'

'Do you live here in Birmingham?'

'Yes, in the town.'

'So you know the big motorway junction,

Spaghetti Junction?'

'Yes, Daddy gets cross at it because so many cars mean it's always busy and slow.'

'Exactly. Well a new road is being built soon. It's part of the motorway, but separate. It's going to be called the M6 Toll Road, because people will have to pay to use it. That's what Toll means. It will take a lot of the traffic away from Spaghetti Junction altogether.

'These books,' he put his hand on the container, 'and yours if you pop it in there with the others, will be pulped down and used to help fasten together the Tarmac and asphalt that makes the top layer of the road surface. The recycling company wants two and a half million of our damaged books. They need about forty-five thousand books for every mile of road that's going to be built.'

'And books can do that?'

'It's been tried before in other countries, and it seems to work. The pulp is very good for absorbing the noise, so it makes the road quieter, and also it lets the rain through gradually, so the road won't get flooded.

'Perhaps when you're old enough to drive you may go down that road, knowing that you're driving over your book.'

Kirsten nodded and placed her damaged book gently into one of the skips. 'There you go book, go and build a road.'

Uppy Downies

Have you ever come back with just the right response to what someone said? I mean immediately, at the critical moment rather than half an hour later or at half past two the next morning?

No? Me neither, until this one time when I did, and boy, did it feel good.

Walking the dog every morning, I tend to change the route for interest; different things for me to look at, different smells for the dog to sniff. The tracks and byways we normally take get very muddy in bad weather, and so I have a little plan. On days when it has been particularly wet, like the day in question, I do what I think of as Uppy Downies. This involves walking up and down the small roads that link the high road at the top of the hill, with the major thoroughfare at the bottom. This way the dog and I can do a lot of Uppy Downies, all eight of them until the two major roads converge at the petrol station, or just a few. Either way the dog stays cleaner than would otherwise be the case.

On this particular morning it had rained heavily throughout the night before, but by daybreak the sun was feebly breaking through. Not a day for walking up unmade lanes, across village greens and through a farmyard, so definitely an Uppy Downy morning.

As we were coming to the end of our walk, with only the estate of modern houses to pass through before reaching home, we rounded a ninety degree bend on a road called Brundell Drive, as a car pulled up beside us, heading in the same direction. The passenger window opened and the driver leaned across waving an A-Z.

'Can you tell me where Easedale Close is?'

That was it. Just like that. No *Please,* no *Sorry to trouble you*, no *Excuse me*, just the bald question in a strident voice. I have heard that our opinion of someone forms within the first eleven seconds in their company, and I formed my opinion of her all right! However, I'm a polite sort of person, so I responded.

'You need to turn round, and go back round this first ninety degree bend. Then Brundell Drive makes another sharp bend to the right, but ignore that and instead carry straight on. It looks as though it should be a continuation of the road you're already on, but in fact it's Dilworth Avenue. You can tell by the road markings, the dotted white lines, and the street signage shows you the change of name at that point.

'Easedale Close is the first cul-de sac on the right off Dilworth Avenue. In fact it's the only road that turns off Dilworth at all.'

I was ready to leave her to it, and carry on walking home, when the imperious tone came once again, and for a second or two took my breath away.

'No, it isn't. I've just come that way.'

And then it came to me. I could of course, have been very rude at this stage but got a great deal more satisfaction from slapping back quite politely,

'Okay. Well, of the two of us, I'm the one who has lived round here for years, and you're the one who's lost. So good luck finding it anywhere else.' Then I walked off.

They say that little things amuse little minds; I think they're right and I must have a very little mind indeed because that small interaction had me smiling for the rest of the day.

Cat Napping

I must have been lying here for an hour or more now. Well, not exactly lying; more scrunched up in this small space in between the bed and the cupboard. The clock says it's nearly three am, but I'm not sure exactly what time I fell out of bed. If my Lola was still here she'd have sorted it, got me back into bed or, as a last resort, phoned our daughter for help. But I'm on my own now, except for the cat.

Mr Tibbles was Lola's cat really, but when she passed away he transferred his demands to me. They're not loyal in the same way dogs are. Mr Tibbles is just sitting on Lola's dressing table, I suspect wondering whether this debacle is going to interfere with him getting his breakfast on time. If no-one rescues me and I die here he'll probably eat me. I heard that they do that if they get desperate, but hopefully it won't come to that.

I can only remember once before ever falling out of bed and that was when I was a child. We were on holiday somewhere, staying in a flat. There were bunk beds in our room and, being the elder, I got first dibs at sleeping on the top. There were no duvets in those days, but sheets and blankets tucked in. The problem I think was that although these bunks were pushed up against a wall, that wall was on the other side of the bed from the one at home. We never thought to change ends; bunk beds were an adventure, we just got into bed as they were.

In the middle of the night, possibly about the same time as now, I must have rolled over too far. Bunk beds I think are narrower than a regular single bed and that may have been part of the problem. Anyway, I rolled right out. I was so deeply asleep I didn't wake up until I hit the floor, which possibly saved me from being hurt because I was still so relaxed. I landed sort of on my hands and knees. I wonder what the people in the downstairs flat thought of a thud in the early hours of the morning. The noise woke my brother and the two of us just laughed.

I'm not laughing this morning. It's really quite cold now. I tried to stretch over to get the phone, but it's well out of reach. If I could have got it I would have called on Joe, my neighbour. He's a strong guy and kind; he'd haul me out of here like a rag doll. He'd laugh of course, but who could blame him for that? I'd have to buy him a pint as a thank you, but he'd throw me back in bed like I was as light as a feather, and my daughter need never know what an idiot I am.

If I do survive this I'm going to be in so much trouble. My daughter's going to want to know a) how I managed to fall out of the bed I've slept in for years, b) how I managed to land in this position: wedged between the base of the divan and the fitted wardrobes, and c) why I wasn't wearing my alarm button round my neck. The stupid thing is I doubt I could have reached the alarm button anyway from this position, but she probably wouldn't believe that. She was here visiting me the first time the company phoned to check that it was working okay. They do that periodically, but I said to them that in order to check it I'd have to go and get it; it was by the bed. The person on the phone explained very politely that I should wear it all the time; that was the whole point. My daughter then explained, less politely, that it was a waste of money paying for the monthly contract if I wasn't going to use it properly.

I'd got really cold lying here. I'm only wearing my pyjamas, but now I've managed to yank at the edge of the duvet a bit and part of it's sort of flopped in a heap on top of me. It did the job because I dozed off again, even though I'm still wedged. I can't see the clock at all now because the part of the duvet that's still scrunched up on the bed is blocking my view. I've tried to move it, but it's like wrestling with a giant marshmallow with one hand tied behind your back. Time's getting on though. I can see daylight now and I can hear the central heating pipes creaking, so it's either switching itself on at seven o'clock, or switching itself off at eight. I thought of banging on the wall, but that's the trouble with living in a detached bungalow, I'd only be banging on the side of my own garage. Nobody would hear.

Just as I was thinking about banging I heard someone banging on the front door. I tried to shout, but I'm so doubled up and half buried under the duvet that it came out as a feeble little croak and the banging soon stopped. I'm beginning to get hungry now. I'm eyeing the cat up, in the same way he's doing to me. I suspect if we're put to the test that he'll win.

Suddenly there's more banging on the door, and the bedroom is full of people. My daughter, a police constable and two paramedics, who haul me out of my embarrassing position. It takes the three of them to get me upright. They check me over and declare that no harm has been done, although I might be a bit bruised in a few hours. My daughter makes breakfast, feeds the cat, admonishes me about the alarm button, then waits for her husband to arrive to construct a sort of crate thing to block up the gap where I'd got myself wedged.

It doesn't look very elegant, but as she said, neither does an old man in his pyjamas, half-sitting, half-lying, half-under a duvet on the bedroom floor.

She sells Sea Shells

She sells Sea Shells on the Sea Shore.
The Shells she sells are Sea Shells I'm sure.

Do you remember that rhyme from childhood? Probably you do, but do you know who it was about?

Imagine if you will a poor family who lived by the sea in the beautiful Dorset town of Lyme Regis. Richard Anning and his wife Mary had ten children, although only two of them, Mary and Joseph, survived to adulthood. In fact young Mary herself, who was born in 1799, had a lucky escape from death when, at just fifteen months of age, she was taken outdoors with her family and a host of other townsfolk to watch a travelling circus. It seems unclear who was carrying the baby Mary that day but when a thunderstorm battered the area, legend has it that this unfortunate person was struck by lightning and killed outright.

Mary, her parents and brother lived on in Lyme Regis, and as children the two of them supplemented the family's meagre income by finding and selling *Curiosities* as she called them, that they dug up on the shore.

Mary was full of ideas. She built up layers of shellac, a naturally occurring resin, on a base of felt, to fashion what was possibly the first protective hard hat. This she used for safety as she chipped away at the beach and at the bottom of the unstable cliffs in search of the curiosities we now call fossils.

Her little terrier Tray, who accompanied her on her fossil-hunting expeditions, was less well protected. He was killed under a landslide of the Lyme Regis cliffs. Such movement within the cliffs continues today, with the last significant landslide observed at Black Ven, the Eastern cliffs of the town in November 2021, although smaller landslips are a common occurrence.

The death of her father in 1810 incentivised the young Mary, and at the age of 12 she discovered the first Ichthyosaurus skeleton. She went on, over the years, to reveal the first complete Plesiosaurus and Britain's first flying reptile, the Pterodactylus.

The Jurassic coast of Dorset is unique in that there are laid down successive layers from the Triassic, Jurassic and Cretaceous Ages, covering 185 million years of history. For this reason Mary's finds were of significant scientific interest although there was a good deal of ridicule at this eccentric single young woman, and initial scepticism as to whether her finds were all genuine.

It is likely that the rhyme *She Sells Sea Shells on the Sea Shore* was coined as a mockery of her work, as if she was doing nothing more than finding bits on the beach and selling them on as mementos to gullible visitors. But gradually word got around and as her finds could be compared and verified with other scientists' – male scientists' – work, she gained in credibility.

The majority of her important finds ended up in museums, particularly the Natural History Museum, but the Anning family was too poor for these finds to be just given away, even to a prestigious museum. Fortunately Mary's activities had drawn the attention of Lieutenant Colonel Thomas Bird, a rich man who purchased many of her significant finds himself and then donated them to various museums. Thus it was Bird who was given the credit, whilst Mary continued to make ends meet and help her mother and brother by selling off her smaller finds, such as the ammonites that are still prolific on the Dorset coast today.

Mary Anning died unmarried in 1847, when she was forty-seven years old and still relatively unknown outside her own circle. During the final ten years of her life she was recognised with an annuity from the British Association for the Advancement of Science; and then in 1846 she was made the first honorary member of Dorset County Museum. Her obituary was noted in the journal of the Geological Society, a male stronghold that was not to admit women to its membership for another fifty years.

Since society has become more enlightened about the part women can play in science, it has been suggested that the fossils recovered by Mary played no small part in contributing to the theory of evolution put forward by Charles Darwin. In 2010 she was eventually listed by the Royal Society as one of the ten most important British women to influence the history of science, but sadly to many people in this country her name and achievements are still relatively unknown.

Happy Birthday to Me

Where did you spend your fourteenth birthday? How did you celebrate? I bet you can't remember, can you? It's not one of the more memorable ones, fourteen, but I remember exactly where I was, and for good reason.

We had been on holiday and the flight home was scheduled for the Friday afternoon, the day before my birthday. To celebrate we were going to the cinema on the Saturday evening. With it being back to school on Monday we had made no other plans, fortunately. It would have been awkward if tons of friends were coming round to help me celebrate, because I wasn't there.

Late on the Friday evening we piled onto the plane in the Mediterranean sunshine, sorry to be saying goodbye to our favourite resort for another year. We seemed to sit on the tarmac for an inordinately long time in the heat, then there was an announcement from the pilot that there would be a short delay and we would all have to disembark.

'That doesn't sound good,' was Dad's pronouncement, 'if it's only a short delay, surely we could stay on board?' Nobody seemed to have any answers.

We sat around in the now nearly-deserted airport until it was so late that we knew we would not be flying until the following day. In any group of people I suppose there is always one loud-mouth who feels the need to explain to the rest what is going on. We were told by our loud-mouth that there were regulations about night flights over residential areas so they would probably put us up overnight. Eventually we were joined by a harassed-looking airline rep. We were to be taken by bus to a resort half an hour from the one where we had spent our holiday, and twenty minutes from the airport. Or at least, it would have been twenty minutes had we all been going to the same place.

First we had to wait for all our baggage to be off-loaded; clearly this plane was going nowhere. Then all two hundred of us were loaded onto a fleet of coaches and transferred to a number of hotels along the coast. Evidently nowhere had accommodation sufficient to take us all at virtually no notice, and we made several stops before we arrived at what looked to be a rather downmarket hotel on the main road adjacent to a couple of noisy bars, where our names were amongst those read out. I suppose beggars can't be choosers and finding accommodation for a planeload of holidaymakers can't be easy. We were given food, and each had a bed so that was to be thankful for. On the way to the coaches our loud-mouthed fellow traveller had explained that there had developed a crack in the windscreen of the plane, which was only discovered during their pre-flight checks. A tiny crack but nevertheless, as my Dad said, he wouldn't have fancied flying in a plane with that sort of problem. I told him I wouldn't fancy flying in a plane with any sort of problem, and we went off to our respective beds.

So far I haven't named our group loud mouth, as I thought of him. Derek was a middle-aged man holidaying with his wife, who was very quiet, perhaps it was a self-preservation thing. It was Derek who had found out what was wrong with the plane and shared the information as well as a lot of other random information. I heard my parents using terms like know-all and attention-seeker, and he certainly did seem to be at the hub of everything; even getting a sing-song going on the coach.

After the hotel we had stayed at all week, the food at our stop-over seemed very mediocre to us but Derek had spent some time telling us how great it was when we down for breakfast. As I said before, the hotel weren't counting on a massive influx of additional guests. Derek and his wife had eaten breakfast and were going for a swim. He had been told that we wouldn't be collected until at least mid-morning and that we should keep an eye open for a notice posted in the foyer. He and his wife were making the most of this wonderful accommodation and pool, so he said. Why didn't we join them in the lovely-looking pool? We'd already looked at the pool and decided not to bother. I suspect my mum was about to tell him that it was my birthday, but I gently shook my head and she took the hint. For some reason I was reluctant to let this loud stranger know my business.

All the way on the coach back to the airport, via the other hotels, Derek was waxing lyrical about what a marvellous hotel we'd been housed in overnight, how he wished they could be upgraded like that every holiday, and my parents and I just looked at each other. I think it was probably the first time I realised that other people didn't necessarily enjoy the luxurious holidays we were used to. I wondered what he would make of the hotel where we had spent the last fortnight.

As we were waiting in the airport lounge for the flight to be called my mum mentioned to me that we wouldn't be able to go to cinema as planned because of the delay, but maybe we could pick it up the following weekend. Derek of course was standing right behind us and inserted himself into the conversation. What a shame it was to just spend my birthday at airports and on a plane and missing out on a planned cinema trip. He wanted to know how old I was, and I was quite relieved when he and his wife wandered off to talk to someone else.

It wasn't long before the light came on and boarding began. Derek, of course, was sitting directly in front of us on the plane. As we were all settling down before take-off he disappeared for a while. I wondered whether he had gone in search of alternative seats, but he was soon back.

We had been in the air for about half an hour when an announcement came from the pilot, 'Ladies and Gentlemen, we have a VIP sharing the flight to Manchester with us this afternoon,' and then he gave my name!

You could have knocked me down with a

feather. I don't know whether I was more delighted or embarrassed. 'A very special traveller, who is fourteen years old today. We cannot of course light candles on board the aircraft, but we have a cake and I want you to join in helping making it a very happy birthday.'

Then a plane full of nearly two hundred people, led by Derek of course, who had organised the cake, sang Happy Birthday just for me. Derek then led them in Jolly Good Fellow, and Hip Hip Hooray, and then everybody clapped.

I think perhaps I had misjudged Derek. His life wasn't our life; his standards weren't our standards, but he was a genuinely kind chap to a youngster he'd never met and would never meet again. He certainly made my fourteenth birthday one I'll never forget.

Lucky Heather

Lucky heard her mother that morning before she saw her. 'Rabbits, Rabbits, Rabbits.' That was all, but her mother was as reliable as any calendar. On the first day of every month she would go through this small ritual thus, she said, guaranteeing that she would receive a gift before the month was ended. When she was a child Lucky had many times tried to test this theory, but always lost interest a few days in, and by the time she was a teenager she decided that as it did nobody any harm and seemed to make her mother feel better, she would leave well alone.

Lucky, whose real name was Heather, had been told by her father that her mother had always been very superstitious. Years ago there had been quite a battle between her mother and the Post Office. The couple were moving onto a new housing estate when newly married, and allocated only a plot number until the estate was finished, the roads named, and house numbers determined. The alignment of properties dictated that their house number would be number thirteen. Her mother had then requested of the Post Office that, as thirteen was known to be an unlucky number, their house number should not be thirteen but rather it should be changed to 11a. Not surprisingly the Post Office refused, and some terse correspondence had passed between the two of them until her mother had been forced to back down. Even now occasionally a circular would arrive addressed to number 11a.

It was hard for Lucky to turn her back on all her mother's eccentric beliefs. She knew that her mother had acquired their black cat, Sooty to bring them luck. She knew she had been named Heather because white heather is a lucky plant. She supposed that she was fortunate not to be named Clover or something equally bizarre. She had been drip-fed since infancy with such family rules as avoiding walking under a ladder, not putting shoes on the table and other less logical edicts. To her mind walking under a ladder was not advisable anyway. There could be someone up there with a pot of paint, a length of drainpipe or just a bad case of vertigo. Similarly putting shoes on the table, even new shoes, seemed a gross thing to do. Many of her mother's rules though, bore no such scrutiny.

'Have you got your lucky rabbit's foot? You can never have too much help in these circumstances.' The rabbit's foot, which had not been so lucky for the rabbit, was tucked away in Lucky's bag out of sight.

'Yes Mum, and I'm wearing my St Christopher.'

For today Lucky was going to an interview for a new job; a job she really wanted. Had the interview been held on the thirteenth of the month Lucky would possibly not have gone. If it had been for Friday thirteenth she definitely would not have been allowed to go; it would not have been possible. Her mother would barely even get out of bed on what was, supposedly, the unluckiest date on the calendar. She would be appalled at the idea of Lucky going for an interview for a new job on that date.

Coming out of the front door, her umbrella still tightly furled, woe betide anyone who put up one of those bad boys indoors, the first thing she saw was a single magpie perched on the fence post. It was instinctive to look around for his mate, but he seemed to be alone and as the first drops of rain fell on her now-open umbrella, she saw a rainbow over the city rooftops. Wondering whether the bad fortune foretold by a single magpie cancelled out the good fortune of the rainbow, she closed the front door, complete with its horseshoe knocker, and decided that it was too wet to walk into town. She headed for the bus stop, resisting the instinct to avoid stepping on the cracks in the pavement. The bus of course was a number thirteen. More auspicious would have been the number seven, but unfortunately the offices where the interview was to take place were on the wrong side of the city.

The interview seemed to go well. Lucky had been sent some information beforehand, including a triangular diagram showing the structure of the company: CEO at the pinnacle, and down in layers to the canteen staff and cleaners at the bottom. She had inverted the triangle and pointed out that the workers should be at the top. They would, after all, be missed first if the lavatories blocked, the stationery wasn't ordered on time, or the lunches weren't made. After a slight pause it seemed to meet with approval, and she was invited to join the board members in the canteen for lunch.

One of them turned to her, 'Off the record Heather, you will be receiving an offer. We had in mind another candidate until this morning, but she was, on reflection, far too immature. She was concerned about the starting date being the thirteenth. Said it was unlucky. To be honest, in running a professional business we have no time to lose focus to someone's ideas like that. I doubt she would have inverted our triangle and challenged us with it. Sometimes Heather, you have to make your own luck.'

And that was it. No matter how superstitious her mother was about black cats and breaking a mirror and all the rest, this job was a tremendous opportunity for her.

'Starting on the thirteenth would be no problem for me,' she said confidently, and she meant it. She didn't even need to cross her fingers behind her back as she spoke.

From now on Heather would make her own luck.

The Crows' Nest

I said to my mate Maggie, 'These humans think they're the cleverest, far cleverer than we are, but they're not. Not by a very long way, and just look at the size of their heads – huge.'

When I say '*We*' I mean Corvids. You may not know that word, even though it is one you humans made up, but you'll certainly recognise us when I say Maggie and I are Magpies, and we have some close friends and neighbours, the Crows. The Ravens live just across the way. 'Imagine,' I tell Maggie, 'if we had heads and brains the size of humans. We'd be ruling the world, not them, and making a much better job of it too.'

It was a frequent refrain. I don't think Maggie listens anymore, she just smiles with her head on one side when I pause as if she's agreeing with me. Well, I'll show her. You just fly this way with me, and I'll show you too.

Here we are. Now this massive building here is called a hospital. We used to love to perch along the parapet, that's the little wall you can see around the edge of the roof. We liked it there because this side of the building gets the sun and we're sheltered from the worst of the rain. I know we live outside and happily so, but really – nobody needs a soaking wet bed when they retire for the night; except perhaps a fish.

Also, even in the winter it keeps quite warm. I suppose they have lots of machines and lights and stuff that have to be left on all the time in a hospital, so it never really freezes, even though it's quite high. I guess this because of the buzzy thing that the humans call the generator and how it's always humming away to itself.

The problem from the humans' point of view is that we, like every other creature under the sun including them, have to poop to get rid of our waste. When we sit in a line along the front parapet, we tend to poop down onto the patio, over the hospital's front door and past the front windows. And the humans don't like it! It's a hospital for goodness' sake, they're far more likely to catch something in there, than out here from our guano. That's the proper name for bird poop, guano.

There were endless of meetings about us. Ones with the windows open we could hear what was said; we always have some look-outs as a safety measure. We could have given those humans lots of advice about how to limit the problem, but of course nobody consulted us. Our forebears (or should I saw forecrows?) have roosted here for generations, probably since the building was first built and found to be so suitable.

Last year the humans took the drastic step of protecting the whole of the parapet, right the way round all four sides of the hospital building with lots of long metal spikes that make it impossible for us to perch.

We live in Antwerp, a beautiful city and there are trees. The hospital is fronted with a garden area containing quite a few of them, but there is a problem with corvids nesting in trees; there is such a lot of competition from other birds. Nearly all the breeds wanted to roost in the trees, and we had been doing them a favour by using the hospital roof. That way there was room for all of us.

When the spikes were fitted we started to use the trees to build our nests, and found that some of the other birds got really nasty. I can't blame them in one way; they're just trying to survive, the same as we are, but we came in for quite a lot of victimisation. Our nests were targeted for destruction. Some birds removed the little roofs we fit to keep our eggs and chicks dry; others stole the twigs and sticks we had carefully gathered. As I said, there weren't that many trees, and so not many sticks, so we were keen to keep what we had. I know it sounds very unkind but nature can be like that. My role is to look after crows first, then I'll look after other birds if I can, but definitely crows first. That applies to all types of birds, so they do understand.

Strangely, in taking one step towards solving our problem, we actually also made progress in a way we didn't expect.

A meeting of crows is called a Murder, which is most unfortunate and very unfair, but the moniker was decided by the humans and we have to put up with it. We had a meeting. The Murder convened and decided that, having built our nests in the trees we could *liberate* some of those spikes and use them in our nests as protection.

It worked a treat. None of the other birds were prepared to mess with those metal spikes and we're dextrous enough to incorporate them in our nests, pointy end outwards, and also to fashion the little roofs we put over our nests to keep them dry.

We needed loads and loads of spikes but they were easy enough to free up. Our beaks are very strong and once we got the hang of the twist and pull action needed to release them there was soon a regular flotilla of spikes being brought back to the nearest trees to help with our constructions.

We needed so many spikes that the second benefit soon became evident, in that large sections of the parapet facing the gardens were completely stripped of their spikes, and so some of us were able to go back to roosting, and even building nests along the warmth of the parapet once again.

Not surprisingly it didn't take long for the humans to twig (if you'll excuse the pun) to what was going on. It all came to light when a patient, who was clearly bored sitting in a hospital bed all day, noticed that we were taking, not stealing, the long spikes that the humans had placed all along the edge of the parapet. I'm glad that we gave him something to watch, but he really didn't need to report it.

One day there were strange humans around here most of the day. Climbing ladders, hanging out of upper storey windows, which is stupid. They have what seem like massively heavy cameras hanging around their necks too. They are neither as agile as we are, nor can they fly. I was a while wondering what had triggered this incursion into our lives, then Chris Crow told me that he had heard something that might give a clue. Through an open window of the hospital where we all live he had heard that thing called a radio news broadcast giving away our latest strategy for survival.

It clearly stated that we had been stealing, stealing! That got me riled up for a start. Surely everything that seems to belong to nobody and can be picked up and carried away is up for grabs? The point is that these people announced that we have been stealing the protective spikes that they have been putting up on their buildings to stop us nesting. All we have done is appropriate their technique and used it for our own ends.

The meetings started again, with the *Murder* of humans involved in discussions about how to deal with what, to them, was a problem. Then one day a green van arrived and parked outside the hospital's front door. A big crane somebody called a cherry-picker was raised up and two people, also dressed in green, came and started measuring the roof, and the top floor windows and goodness knows what else. It looked for a time very much as if the spikes were going to be replaced, and so they were. This time though it was different. Our parapet was left clear, and we could continue to perch as we used to. The new spikes, which seemed to be much tougher than the old ones, were fastened to the outer edges of a transparent canopy, which was fitted underneath the parapet and over the top bank of windows. This meant that our poop would land on this canopy.

On the day that it was first fitted, another sunny day when the windows were open we heard people talking inside. One of them was asking a nurse what it was for, and the nurse was explaining. I listened very carefully and then later reported back to the murder. The idea is that our guano will be gathered up from time to time from the canopy, and would then be used as fertiliser, to feed all the trees in the town, and so help the other birds.

There would be no mess outside the door of the hospital. The guano would be cleared regularly and the canopy cleaned down, and all the birds would be left to roost in peace.

Based on a true article from New Scientist magazine July 2023

A False Impression

The judge at the Old Bailey listened impassively to the assembled company, occasionally making notes in immaculate calligraphy as he had been taught. It was hot in the courtroom, a fly buzzed relentlessly, constantly missing the few opened windows in favour of those that remained firmly shut. The atmosphere was soporific but the old man was determined not to miss any detail of this case. It was the most unusual that had ever been brought under his jurisdiction, a case of murder no less. After the jury had been sworn in – all men of course, women would not be allowed on juries for another sixteen years, the indictment was read out. A *Not Guilty* plea was made and the judge tuned back in as the prosecuting counsel, Mr Beaverbrook, got to his feet.

'Your lordship, gentlemen of the jury; it is alleged that on the eleventh day of September in the year 1903' he intoned, 'The defendant, Mr Archibald Montague, of 7 Clutterbridge Avenue, Highgate Wood in the City of London, made his way by hansom cab to the home of his friend and business associate Mr de Klerk. There he ate an evening meal with his acquaintance, whom he then killed. The prosecution intends to bring forward evidence to support this claim.' Archibald Montague listened, shaking his head, pondering on the events that had brought him to this point in his life. A life that may soon end on the gallows.

As the details were relayed to the jury, Montague recalled that evening perfectly well. It was the day on which he had expected his mother and sister to have left home to begin their holiday in the south of France, and for their Henley-on-Thames house to be empty. Before he and his wife had chance to sit down for their evening meal – necessarily of cold cuts as it was the cook's day off – a telegram had arrived from his sister. The telegram read:

MOTHER'S PLANS CHANGED DUE TO SICKNESS STOP HOLIDAY CANCELLED STOP PLEASE COME SOONEST STOP MOTHER FADING FAST STOP

Mr Montague, much upset, had declined his wife's offer to make up a light repast to sustain him on the journey, saying that he would have to leave at once to be sure of catching the through train to Oxford. He would eat there, before picking up a hansom cab out to Henley. As his wife fetched his hat, coat, gloves and cane he screwed up the telegram in annoyance and threw it on the embers of the fire, where the flames curled and blackened around it, reducing it to ash. His last words on leaving the house were: 'I doubt I'll be back tonight. Don't forget to lock up before you retire.'

Mrs Montague confirmed the events and the conversation as her husband described it. She was much overcome as a witness, dabbing her eyes frequently with a silk handkerchief.

*   *   *

The case proceeded. No hansom cab driver could be found who recalled dropping off Archibald Montague at de Klerk's. However it was a fine night and the prosecution maintained that he may have walked to preserve his anonymity. Mr de Klerk had definitely shared his evening meal with someone. Two used dinner plates were in the kitchen, two empty wine glasses still on the table, alongside the remains of grapes and cheese that had evidently followed the meal. At the place facing the one where Mr de Klerk's body was found, there remained a part-eaten piece of cheese on a dessert plate. In this cheese someone, presumably Mr de Klerk's final guest, had clearly left the imprint of his bite mark. Crucially those teeth marks were later found to match those made by the false teeth belonging to the defendant, Mr Archibald Montague. It seemed an open and shut case.

Mr Fitzherbert responded for the defence, maintaining his client's innocence.

'After the receipt of the telegram that evening my client, much concerned for his mother's health, departed as soon as possible for Henley. As he expected he was able to hail a hansom cab within a hundred yards of his front door, many cabs plying their trade along the major routes and the affluent streets of Highgate during the evenings. My client made good progress. Deciding against stopping in Oxford, his appetite being diminished by concern for his mother's condition, he hailed another cab to take him directly to the Henley family home. There he found the house in darkness, and his repeated rapping on the door brought no response. The home, where his aged mother was purportedly on her death bed, was empty. Using his own key he let himself in to ponder his next steps. It did not appear that the house had been left in a hurry. Nothing was in disarray and his mother's luggage was missing, as he would have expected had the holiday proceeded as planned.

'He poured himself a tot of whisky, then sat in the living room. The next thing he knew it was coming daylight. The alcohol, worry and lack of food had taken their toll and he had been asleep for several hours. Checking his pocket watch he found that it was six thirty in the morning, during which time nobody had arrived at or left the house.

'His mother had flatly refused to have a telephone installed, believing these new-fangled gadgets to be unnecessary, and stating that they listened to what one was saying, so he had no choice but to lock the house up and walk down to the nearest village. There he hailed a cab and retraced his steps of the previous evening. His wife suggested to him that he had been the victim of a prank, although had no suggestion as to who should have conceived of such an idea, nor why. Later, he received the news that his friend and business associate, Mr de Klerk had, the previous evening been murdered at his home.'

Mrs Agnes Hopkins, a skivvy from Henley, was called to the stand to begin her testimony. Totally unfazed by the occasion and wearing a new bonnet she had bought especially, she spoke with surprising clarity and certainty.

'On that evening I was summoned by my employer, Mrs Russell, what lives in the property nearest to that of Mrs Montague and her daughter in Henley. Mrs Russell was with child and her pains had begun. She sent me to the village to fetch the midwife, entrusting me with twenty whole pounds to secure an 'ansom cab to bring us both back.

'My youngest, Alfred, is a cab driver, and was waiting, as I expected, for custom outside Henley town 'all. I gave him the money, told him to take me first to the midwife's 'ouse and then to bring us both back to Mrs Russell. The babby weren't born till the morning, and at seven o'clock Alfred came to collect me and take me back 'ome for some breakfast. The midwife was waiting with Mrs Russell till the wet nurse arrived.'

Alfred Hopkins, looking uncomfortable in his starched collar and his Sunday suit, took the stand, confirming what his mother had said.

'I did see summat else,' he said to the assembled company when asked, 'As I left, havin' dropped off my mam and the nurse lady, there was this 'ansom cab trying to turn out of Mrs Montague's driveway.' He went on to describe this as *not the easiest as it's a sharp corner,* and so he had quite a wait. He took a good look at the cabbie, who was someone he didn't recognise. 'Prob'ly one of them what hangs round at the station in Oxford for richer pickin's than we normally get in Henley. Someone told me there's over ten thousand 'ansom cabs around just in London. I can't know all them cabbies.

'I saw the cab's passenger too, what entered the house with a key from his own pocket.' He looked around at his appreciative audience, 'It was Mr Montague what arrived and let himself in.'

There was a loud gasp and the judge banged his gavel in disapproval. Asked how he could be so sure, Alfred confirmed that he was quite positive. Prior to his marriage Mr Archibald Montague had lived at that house with his mother and sister, and was well-known locally. Alfred, who was also a chimney sweep when called upon, had attended the Montague wedding in his sweep's garb as a good luck charm. He knew all the Montagues. Asked whether the passenger he had seen was in court that afternoon, he confirmed that the passenger was the gentleman in the dock, Mr Archibald Montague.

*   *   *

EARLY 1904: AND NOTHING BUT THE TRUTH

Five months later, the Montagues of Highgate Wood were again the centre of proceedings at the Old Bailey, but this time it was Mrs Montague, Archibald's wife, who was in the dock. Her husband was a key witness for the prosecution, and his mother and sister lent him their support from the viewing gallery.

Having recapped for the jury's benefit the findings from the previous trial, the prosecuting counsel, one Mr Raymond spoke up.

'We now consider the facts of the case before you, gentlemen of the jury. Once her husband had left the house bound for Henley that evening exactly as he had stated, Mrs Montague first ensured that the telegram, which she herself had arranged to be delivered to him earlier, was thoroughly destroyed and the fire was extinguished. That way it could never be established that it had originated in Highgate Wood and not in Henley. She gave her husband time to walk to the major road, and in the street she then hailed a cab of her own. She asked that the driver set her down at the corner of Golders Green, from where she walked the few hundred yards to Hampstead and the home of her husband's business acquaintance, who was, unbeknownst to her husband, Mrs Montague's lover.'

Sensing a scandal, the jurymen leant forward, the better to hear any juicy snippets about this upper class couple that were to be told. They heard that some two years previously Mr de Klerk has advised Archibald Montague about the opportunity to invest in a South African diamond mine near Kimberley. Discussions and negotiations about the mine had been conducted over a number of dinners at the Montague home, at which Mrs Montague had acted as hostess. The diamond enterprise had proved extremely successful and yielded Mr Montague a significant dividend at the year end. According to Mrs Montague a large sum of this money had been removed from the bank's safe keeping, and had been pocketed by her husband for his own pleasure. Some had been spent on new clothes, new spectacles and new false teeth. Much of it, his wife suspected, had been set aside for him to spend on other women.

The defence counsel made a brave showing. Why, he had asked, would Mrs Montague want Mr de Klerk dead? Far from being her lover as her husband suspected, she barely knew the man. What reason would she have to try and implicate her husband in such a terrible crime? But his efforts were futile. Her husband could not be in two places at once. He had been identified by someone who knew him well in Henley and so could not have been in Hampstead. He had gone free at the end of that previous hearing, totally exonerated, to return not to his home in London, but with his mother and sister to Henley.

'This is the story of a woman scorned.' maintained the prosecutor, 'She felt that her husband was moving away from her, possibly about to abandon her altogether for another woman, and she took steps to ensure his demise before that could happen. She and Mr de Klerk had grown quite fond of one another during the hospitality he had enjoyed at her home, and he was soon offering this hostess hospitality in return, of a more intimate kind. But he was becoming more and more insistent in his pursuit of her and more reckless about secrecy, putting her reputation and therefore her livelihood at risk. She decided that he was expendable to achieve her ends.

'On the night in question, Mrs Montague arranged for a lad to deliver Mr Montague the telegram, purporting to be from his sister in Henley. She commiserated with him about his mother's plight and agreed that her husband should go at once. She offered to make him a light meal for the journey. In spite of it being the cook's night off she could surely find him something, but he refused. He would get something, he said, once he reached Oxford.

'Why did she act this way? Because she had grown to distrust her husband, perhaps because of what she perceived to be his meanness and his suspected philandering? Or because she was tired of him, and to kill Mr de Klerk and have her husband hang for the crime of murder would leave her free as a very rich widow?

'The biggest stumbling block to this scenario, gentlemen of the jury, was of course the piece of cheese. A part-consumed wedge of dessert left on the plate at Mr de Klerk's house, which could seemingly have only been left by Archibald Montague, his teeth marks being indisputable. But the false teeth were brand new, bought, as Mrs Montague had previously confirmed, with the proceeds from the recent business transactions in the diamond mine.'

Called to the stand was Mr Montague's prosthodontist. He agreed that Mr Montague had collected his new teeth two days before the murder of Mr de Klerk. However, the patient had complained the following day that they were ill fitting at one point, and had rubbed his gums raw. He had been told to leave out the new set, and use his old ones if they were sufficiently comfortable. The prosthodontist was about to leave on holiday for a week, but would certainly see Mr Montague immediately on his return. An appointment was made and the professional's appointment book was duly shown in court. Mr Montague confirmed that he had indeed been wearing his old teeth that day. He had not felt that his wife would be interested to know this, and so had not mentioned it. He had placed the new set on the bedside cabinet, ready for his appointment a week hence.

It was here that his wife had found them whilst he was occupied elsewhere, in advance of the evening in question, and had used them to deface a piece of cheese from her own kitchen. The remains of this she then took with her to Hampstead and left on the dessert plate opposite the body of her late lover, whom she had just killed.

As the jury watched her face as all this was revealed, it was evident that what she had regarded as the coup de grâce, would be the means of hanging her.

Nobody else knew about the teeth. Nobody certainly knew where her husband had left them. Nobody knew which set was which. The teeth marks in the cheese at Mr de Klerk's could only have been administered by his wife. It transpired and was announced by the prosecuting counsel with a final flourish that there was another point to consider. Mrs Archibald did not know her lover so very well. Mr de Klerk had heartily disliked cheese and never kept it in the house.

As Archibald shook hands with his defence counsel on the courtroom steps, having watched his wife led down to the cells for the final time, he offered his thanks.

'One thing puzzles me,' said his counsel, 'What were you going to do with the money you had drawn out of the bank? Just man to man. If there is another lady involved it's no concern of mine and the case is closed, this is just idle curiosity.'

Montague gave him a wry smile, 'My late father's investments had unfortunately proved far less satisfactory than my own of late. I used some of the money to pay for my mother and sister to go on their holiday to Nice. I had also helped them out with household bills recently. With the remainder I had planned to take my wife on a surprise trip to the Italian Riviera. It was somewhere she often said she would like to visit. I anticipated that that would involve a new wardrobe, and so had set a sum aside for that also.'

'And what will you do now?'

'I will sell the Highgate Wood house. I have come to hate it. I shall move back in to the family home in Henley where I will better be able to help my mother and sister.'

What's in a Name?

Of course it was my fault. It's always my fault according to my partner. She's one of these people who is super-efficient and never seems to make the basic blunders in life that are my stock in trade. Perhaps that's why we generally get along so well together. It happened that the wedding invitation arrived at a time when business was slow – my business that is, Imogen's shifts seemed never to suffer the peaks and troughs that mine did. If anything she just worked harder and harder as time went on. Recently there had been a few staff off work at her place due to illness, and she'd been working long shifts on nights for ten days straight.

Because I was at a bit of a loose end Imogen suggested that I should organise the trip, even though it was her cousin who was getting married. I checked the invitation and searched on line to find the address of the Register Office. It was on Southend High Street, so should be easy enough. There was a pleasant looking hotel a few streets away, so I booked us in and organised the wedding present. We had a fun weekend shopping for outfits, rejecting the outlandish idea of us both dressing as men, in favour of dresses that we could later wear in our respective offices. I arranged appointments at the hairdresser for the day before and reminded Imogen to book the Monday off work so we could make a long weekend of it.

Once the hotel booking was confirmed I checked the travelling times from London, and on the morning of the wedding put the hotel coordinates in the SatNav. One hour twenty minutes was the estimate, loads of time to book into the hotel and change for the ceremony. 'I thought it would take longer than that,' was Imogen's only comment, 'Perhaps if we like the look of it we could go again later in the year.'

'I'd like that.' Nearly all my travelling away from London had been either to Norfolk to see my family, or up towards the Midlands.

Almost as soon as we set off Imogen fell asleep. I took it as a compliment to my driving that she could relax so fully, although it was more likely the result of her only having had a couple of hours sleep in the last twenty four.

One major road looks much like another heading out of London and you have to keep your wits about you driving on a Saturday morning, so apart from Imogen snoring gently beside me the journey was carried out in silence. It seemed like no time at all until we approached Southend. As we slowed in the congestion approaching the city centre Imogen stirred and stretched. She looked out of the car window.

'I thought it was on the coast.' she said gazing over the water to our right at the landmass beyond, 'what's that over there? Is it the Isle of Wight?'

'The Isle of Wight,' I laughed at her, 'I doubt it. It'll be the Isle of Sheppey probably. We're just near the mouth of the Thames.'

Imogen sat bolt upright, 'The Thames? What are we doing near Sheppey? The wedding's just along the coast from Portsmouth.'

'Portsmouth?'

'Yes. Southsea is the next town along. What have you done?' she asked, scrabbling in my handbag for the wedding invitation and the hotel booking as the SatNav announced that we had reached our destination.

'Oh, you clown! The wedding is being held at the Register Office in Southsea High Street, and you have brought us to a hotel near the High Street, Southend-on-Sea.'

She did a quick calculation. 'The ceremony starts in an hour, and we are now two and a half hours away. Oh boy, are you going to have some explaining to do.'

Flaming Katy

Bridget had first met Zac's Granny Katy the December before she and Zak married, and she already seemed incredibly ancient then. It seemed that with the trends of dress and hair, and the mind-set of women such as Granny Katy, they became old before their time.

They had visited her little bungalow, and she had made tea. Proper tea, in a teapot and using a tea strainer, and with milk in a jug. There was a little basin too with lumps of sugar and little tongs, the like of which Bridget had never seen before. They chatted for a while, it was just a duty visit really, and then as they were leaving she had taken Bridget to one side.

'I think you two will be very happy together. I have a little Christmas gift for you.' She had disappeared into the kitchen and returned with a plant. At first Bridget thought it had red flowers, but Granny Katy told her that these were more akin to leaves, and were correctly called bracts. 'It's a poinsettia,' she said, 'one of many Christmas traditions that are difficult to explain. Lots of families have them displayed at Christmas.'

Good manners kick in in these situations. Bridget could hardly say that she didn't like it, didn't want it, and in fact thought it looked rather grotesque, with its non-leaves, non-flowers that were a brilliant red. The reality was that although Bridget didn't much like it at all, not the look of it, nor the texture of these bracts, she was very touched at the gesture. 'How lovely,' she said, carefully not catching Zak's eye, 'that's very kind of you.'

Thereafter every Christmas Granny Katy had given them a poinsettia. Every year it either died quite soon afterwards, or it survived seemingly forever, growing taller, more leggy and scraggy-looking and less healthy than Bridget would have thought possible. It was said in the family that Granny Katy had green fingers. She could put a bare stick in the ground and within a few months it was a beautifully thriving plant. Bridget was the opposite. Give her a beautiful, thriving plant and within a few months she would manage to reduce it to a bare stick.

Whereas Bridget appreciated the gesture and was happy for the poinsettias to put on their showy display for the few weeks they survived, Zak hated them with a passion. He coined the expression Flaming Katy for what he called *These abominations of nature.*

'They're not flowers, they're not leaves. They grow leggy trying to get enough light. They must be forced in extreme conditions to look like that at Christmas at all. They are horrible,' It was at about this time each year, roughly the middle of February, when the poinsettia would be replaced by the Valentine's Day bouquet he had bought for Bridget, and the sad-looking plant could at last be consigned to the compost bin.

When she died Zac's Granny Katy was a very old lady by any criteria. Zak couldn't work out whether she was a hundred and two or a hundred and three, but certainly she had been born at the back end of the nineteenth century, which was difficult to assimilate. He was surprised at how upset he was by her loss.

Bridget had always been the more pragmatic of the couple. A funeral doesn't need to be a sad affair, she had told him. It should be the celebration of a life well lived. Granny Katy was delightful and had a long and fulfilled life. Bridget suggested that they should sit down and consider all the good aspects of it.

On the eve of the funeral they got out old photograph albums and found a CD with footage transferred from ancient cine film. They watched together as she played across their television screen, chasing her many grandchildren on the beaches of their holidays; eating ice-cream at a dog show, and laden with shopping bags one Christmas as she watched different grandchildren confide their deepest secrets to Santa. One scene showed the Christmas table, surrounded by family and friends and they laughed together as they spotted the poinsettia, the Flaming Katy that, even back then, graced the sideboard.

The old lady had managed to fend for herself right up until her final illness; that was something to be grateful for. She had never gone short of money for good food, clothes when she wanted them, holidays while she had been able to enjoy them, and she could always put the heating on if she felt chilly. She had seen all her children and grandchildren grow up healthy and happy, do well in their chosen careers, and the next generation of babies had been her pride and joy. The locker beside her bed when she was finally admitted to hospital was covered in photos of happy groups of young people.

The evening was an enjoyable one of reminiscences, and also learning things about Granny Katy that Zac had not previously known, like what she had done during the war, and her job after leaving school before she married Grandpa. It helped Zac to write the short section of the eulogy that he would present at the funeral.

It was towards the end of the service, as the coffin disappeared behind the closing curtain and sombre music played, that another thought struck Bridget. She squeezed Zac's hand and leaned across to whisper:

'I've thought of another thing to be celebrated about Granny Katy's death. Not for the eulogy though, just between the two of us.'

He looked at her with a weak smile, 'What's that?'

'We won't have to have another Flaming Katy and pretend we love it every Christmas.'

In spite of himself Zac began to giggle. 'I think perhaps we should get ourselves one each year anyway. Just to remember Granny Katy by.'

A Room with a View

There is nothing as dead as dead love. Kim's grandfather had told her this when she went to confide and cry about the final breakdown of her relationship. She told him that she was moving out, and had rented a small flat in the centre of town.

It had been a scramble to move in on the same day as the previous tenant moved out, but he had helped her with some of the lifting. Making him a cup of tea when all the heavy furniture had been moved into position Kim found him admiring a water colour painting she had just propped against the living room wall. He asked whether it was a print or an original.

He'd heard of the artist Don J Gill, said that in fact he was quite well known. The chap had died within the last year or so he told her, and his originals sold for quite a bit of money. He hadn't been a really old man, just in his early seventies. It was sad to hear that he'd passed away. Kim made a mental note to ask her grandad when she visited him later in the week. If she remembered correctly he had bought the painting many years ago from someone selling door-to-door. Perhaps some down and out he felt sorry for. He'd passed it on to her years ago when she said the colour would be a perfect match for her dining room walls.

Her grandfather's memory of acquiring the painting was very clear. He led her into the kitchen and put the kettle on.

'I met the artist, Don, nice man. He came to the door. Initially I didn't understand, and told him I wasn't interested, didn't buy stuff on the doorstep. You know the sort of thing, but he looked so disappointed and said that in that case he'd probably just throw it away, maybe use the frame for something else. He said that it was a shame I'd not even looked at it after all his effort.

'I was a bit taken aback, Kim. I'd expected he'd just try and sell it to someone else, and asked him why would he throw it away. Then he said that it was a painting of my house, where I was living. He'd thought it a beautiful building, which it was, but if I didn't want it then probably nobody else would.'

He paused as he watched her stirring the pot, and then followed her back into the sitting room.

'Of course this was way back. We lived at the big house by the river then, and it was that house he'd painted; our house.'

Her grandfather stirred sugar into his cup as he gazed out of the window, remembering.

'I told him that I hadn't realised, that I'd thought it was just a picture of … well any old house. Then I had a look at it. It was well painted, as you know. I suppose an expert would know that it was not a professional job, but this guy was a gifted amateur and had painted it with feeling. It would look good over the piano in the drawing room, so I asked him how much he wanted for it.

'He said that as long as he could cover his costs, he didn't need more. He'd made the frame himself, and suggested that I'd better change that, although I never did. Then he said ten pounds would cover his materials and a bit for his time. He told me he was a widower and he'd taken up painting as a hobby, not as a job. He'd been told that he needed to relax more when he had a health scare a couple of years earlier, and painting was ideal.

'He'd painted it from a couple of photographs apparently. He wanted me to have those too, said he wouldn't want anyone to think he'd been sneaking around taking photos and up to no good. He really was a nice chap, came in for a cuppa and a chat, and I gave him twenty pounds. I asked him if he'd come back and paint the house from a different angle in the spring, but he never did. I wonder what happened to him.

'One thing I didn't do was change the frame. He'd used that wood because it toned well with the painting's colour combination, but he'd put it together himself and he told me it wouldn't be as strong as a professionally made frame. Have you ever changed it?'

'No, I hung it earlier this week just as it's always been. I like the frame too. Perhaps I need to take a closer look, make sure it's not going to come crashing down.'

When she got home Kim lifted the painting down off the wall to examine it while it was still daylight. It was fortunate that she did. She saw that the framing tape securing the picture had dried out and was no longer safe. Probably the heat from the fire at the other house had loosened it. As she carried it over to the window for a closer look, the whole of the frame seemed to shift and an envelope slid out from between the backing board and the watercolour painting itself, landing on the floor.

Saving this as a treat to explore later, she first checked how she might get the whole thing put together securely, and decided that the painting was an original after all. She really liked it; she would get it fixed and put it back on the wall. She would phone the local framing shop tomorrow and see what they could suggest.

In the meantime she made herself a cup of tea and turned her attention to the envelope. Slid inside it was a will; *the* will of the artist Don J Gill. It was dated the same year as the picture had been painted and seemed to Kim's inexperienced eye to be all in order. It was written on a will form, properly signed and witnessed and dated by two people, neither of whom were named in it. In fact there was only one beneficiary, a John Beaumont. There was no indication about any relationship between the artist and this man, but the will did contain Beaumont's address at the time. Of course this may be well out of date but it was a starting point.

John Beaumont was a few years older than Kim. They met in a local pub and she showed him the will. He stared at it for a long time before he spoke, while she sipped her wine.

'I always knew I was adopted and that he was my birth father. He'd been beginning to make a name for himself as a painter when he died. I'd sort of watched his life from afar, not stalking him, but taking an interest. I knew he had been married, but there were no more children and his wife died young. I have one of his pictures on my wall, but it's just a print.' He exhaled loudly and shook his head,

'I had no idea about this will. I assumed that he just didn't want to know me. I didn't even know for sure whether he was aware of my existence.'

'Perhaps he didn't want to disrupt your new life. He clearly knew you and he knew your address, and he left you everything. That doesn't sound like someone who wasn't interested.'

'It's a shame I won't get to talk to him.'

'You need to do some digging. He might have made a subsequent will, and this one would be worthless then. How long ago did he die?'

'It was in the paper. He died back in February, so not that long really.'

'He tried to persuade my grandad at the time to change the frame on the painting, but we never have. I think perhaps he wanted the will to be found and kept safely; in which case he is unlikely to have made a more recent one. You need to talk to a solicitor.'

Three weeks after their meeting John phoned Kim and asked her to meet him again. He had some information and an idea that he wanted to share with her. They had spoken on the phone a few times during those three weeks, but Kim was keen to see him again and hear his news.

The corner table in the pub was spread with various papers. John had remembered and bought her a glass of white wine.

'I got onto the Wills Registry,' he said, after giving her a peck on the cheek, 'There was no other will ever registered, before or after. I also spoke to a neighbour who was at his funeral. He had told her everything was to go to his boy, but no other details. She didn't like to pry.'

He paused and sipped his pint, 'There's something called Bona Vacantia, *Vacant Goods,* which basically means that if an estate isn't willed to someone, or isn't automatically claimed by someone such as a spouse, then it goes to the crown. They search really hard to find beneficiaries before that happens though, it can take years. The will you found has been proved and is a legally binding document. So all my late father's estate is mine; the house, the paintings everything. It's a bit of a shock.'

'Wow! And what will you do? What's the idea you wanted to share?'

He began to look diffident. 'It seems a bit cheeky asking, you've done such a lot for me already, but I wondered whether you would help me put together an exhibition of his paintings. I don't want something stiff and starchy, but as you said you loved the one you own already. The art gallery in town is receptive to the idea, and I'd like to put a bit about the story of finding the will too; perhaps with some words by you and your grandfather.'

He looked totally animated and she caught the enthusiasm, 'That sounds brilliant! Your print, my painting as a start; whatever other paintings are included in your legacy; something from my grandad; the story about how I came to look in the back of the picture. We could put out a shout on the radio and social media for other paintings we could borrow to go on show. It will be a real tribute to Don J Gill.

Kim realised suddenly that she was enjoying herself, possibly for the first time since her relationship break-up. Now she had something to look forward to. She would get the home-made picture frame professionally repaired, not replaced. It would be a reminder of why the frame was special.

And who knew? As they moved forward on a common mission maybe one day the two works by Gill, John Beaumont's print and her watercolour painting, would share a home together.

Credit Where It's Due

It was a great job and I was very happy there for three years. Then we became victims of our own success. An expansion was announced, involving restructuring and that meant a new manager for me.

Never have I seen the Peter Principle so clearly acted out. My new manager, let's call him Sean, had been a competent operative, not outstanding but a good steady worker who knew his job. With the promotion came a complete change. He was so far out of his depth that his feet couldn't reach the bottom; all he could do was tread water and hope that the rest of us picked up the slack. The change showed in his attitude too. Sean became almost paranoid about his lack of skills being shown up by a team member, and fell into the habit of taking credit for the best work produced by the team, without giving credit to the team member who had produced whatever it was.

Quarterly I was charged with compiling production figures in the form of a presentation, which was given to the members of the board. They would ask questions about anything that was unclear; about projections, about obstacles to achieve what we set out to and so on. It was all standard stuff and nothing very challenging. The Directors were always appreciative of the time I'd spent and the detail I produced.

Sean was jealous. I knew this because as soon as they'd started to praise my work and talk about possible promotion in the future, he'd become very unreasonable and would do anything to try and show me up. Then one quarter, Sean said that he would do the presentation to the Board. No reason was given, he simply asked that I put together the slides of information as usual, and then hand them over for him to present. He was going to deliver it to the Directors as his own work. I wasn't of course required to attend that meeting so I don't know how it went, except that the door opening as the Directors were preparing to leave, had me able to hear a little of the conversation. A Director was asking whether Sean had put the presentation together and Sean said that he had. He was praised for its professionalism as it hadn't been him that did it previously, and he had a grin like the Cheshire Cat when they had gone. He gave me very little feedback, just asked for me to do the same thing for future meetings.

The following quarter was the year end, so the slides were very different. There was more information needed about past performance, and a whole raft of projections about the future, different variables and all sorts of other stuff that needed to be gone into in some detail. Sean should have known this. He had been present at the last year end presentation I had given, so I supposed that he would cope with it. I reminded him that it was more complex and that I was happy to do it, but he just asked me to hand the slides over as before and go back to whatever I should be doing.

The noise of raised voices in the boardroom could be heard from the general office that afternoon. The Directors were asking for clarification, details, percentage breakdowns – all sorts of things and Sean didn't have a clue. He came out of the room and asked me would I please join them, as some of the information on my slides wasn't at all clear. The slides were perfectly clear to anyone capable of understanding and interpreting them but, as I say, the Peter Principle applied.

I smoothed over the ruffled feathers, answered questions and gave the Directors the information they wanted. One Director, Mrs Dawson, asked for a copy of the slides to take away, so she could peruse them more thoroughly in her own time, so I printed a set off for her. I thought, mistakenly, that Sean would be pleased that it was all sorted out satisfactorily. Instead he blew up at me, suggesting that I was after his job and that I had *Deliberately Sabotaged* his presentation to make him look incompetent. Resisting the temptation to say that he was managing to look incompetent all by himself, I asked him what happened now? He had it all worked out. For the next quarter's details I was to compile the slides exactly as I had been doing for years, then I was to schedule a meeting with him to go through them on the morning before the afternoon Board meeting.

By now I was getting a bit fed with Sean's attitude. There was a lot of criticism and no praise from Sean for anyone in the team. Several members were spending their lunchtimes looking at the Situations Vacant column over their sandwiches, which is never a good sign, and I was tempted to join them. Morale was at rock bottom and the quality of work was dropping off because people didn't feel valued. I had to think of something.

The following quarter I put together the slides as requested, along with a little bonus for Sean. In between the twenty four sets of figures in the presentation I inserted a few extras. Nothing unseemly you understand, just a photograph of a gorilla in the jungle, a teddy bear wearing sunglasses, a racing car on the beach, that sort of thing. All fairly innocuous, just out of place in a board meeting. When I went through the presentation with Sean that morning, I managed to successfully skip over the rogue slides so quickly that he didn't notice. He was trying so hard to absorb the information he would need to share that I nearly felt sorry for him. Nearly.

He headed confidently into the boardroom that afternoon, fully primed for the meeting. A thank you for my time would have been appreciated but I decided not to push my luck. I waited by the water cooler for the balloon to go up, and boy, did it go up!

The Chairman of the Board came barrelling out of the room with a red-faced Sean bowing and scraping in his wake.

'Something wrong?' I asked innocently.

'I've never seen such gross incompetence. This fool thinks he's a comedian.'

'I swear sir, I didn't know ...' Sean glared at me, and I shrugged my shoulders – no idea what he was talking about.

'We'll reconvene at four o'clock this afternoon, and you,' the Director pointed to me, 'will come and make sense of this fiasco.'

Sean was incandescent. He accused me of setting him up, but I suggested that we must have been hacked. It must have been someone's idea of a joke.

He threatened me with all sorts of sanctions, 'Don't come looking to me to approve time off for your sports activities any more,' (I was on a county championship amateur sports team,) 'I plan to make your life hell from here on in.' Unfortunately for him, the Chairman of the Board had left the boardroom door ajar, and when he'd finished his angry rant Sean turned to find the directors grouped around the doorway, listening to every word. The Directors said that at the end of my presentation they would like to see Sean in the boardroom to discuss his future.

My presentation went without a hitch and I was told that this would be written into my job description as a key part of my role, and that there may be a promotion opportunity shortly. I was profusely thanked by each of them and Mrs Dawson, who had asked for copies of slides at the previous meeting, came across to me.

'Would you like a copy of these slides?' I asked her.

'Not all of them this time thanks, your explanation was crystal clear. But if you could just get me a copy of the one of the gorilla, my little boy loves gorillas,' and she winked at me.

The Bear and Billet

It was a special occasion. 'After all,' Nell told their young son Noah as she finished icing the cake, with Noah standing on a chair beside her at the kitchen table, 'Daddy doesn't have such a special birthday every day, or even every year.' She took two fancy candles from a paper bag, and carefully placed the three and the zero in amongst the sweet decorations on the top of the cake. 'This is for today. Then tomorrow as a treat, we are going to Chester for the day; a trip in a boat on the river, then afternoon tea in the upstairs café of a posh pub.'

'Going to the posh pub,' echoed Noah, who was more interested in the smarties decorating the cake, and what might happen to those that were unused. He soon found out when Nell placed four of the coloured sweets in front of him, and nodded her approval that he should eat them.

The early part of the day out was a great success. It was years since Nell and Bernard had visited the city, before they married in fact, and the sun shone gloriously as they walked around the Rows, then were transported upstream, spying moorhens, swans and even a kingfisher. Noah loved bouncing around on the steps up the Rows, and was excited on the boat trip. Nell reflected that they were fortunate to have a son with such a sunny temperament. Nothing seemed to curb his excitement. Returning to the pier, they climbed up the short hill to the pub where Nell had booked Afternoon Tea for the three of them, making sure that they understood that Noah was little more than a toddler.

'We serve the teas upstairs in our separate tearooms,' she had been told on the phone. 'You will have to pass through the bar, but then go straight up the stairs. They are quite steep. If you have a buggy with you we will be happy to store it for you behind the bar. It will be quite safe while you enjoy your tea.'

'Oh thank you, no,' she responded, 'Noah's too grown up for the buggy now. He'll be fine.'

Having been thus reassured, Nell was nevertheless quite alarmed when they entered the Bear and Billet, at just how steep and uneven those stairs to the first floor were. They were hidden behind an oak door of the ancient building, which no doubt helped to keep the two parts of the business separate. Noah would never manage those stairs on his own and Bernard lifted him up and carried him carefully against his shoulder.

The little boy was reluctant to be put down, and clung to Bernard's jacket, shaking his head. Bernard prised the child's hands free and placed a very subdued Noah at the tea table. In spite of the lovely selection of goodies on the children's menu

Noah was acting very strangely; staring at the floor, pushing away his orange juice so quickly that it spilled, and barely eating anything of the tasty treats on offer. It seemed to quite upset the waitress that she couldn't tempt him with the various cakes and pastries she offered. It quite took the edge off the outing for the adults as they tried to tempt him with this morsel and that.

They soldiered on through the traditional cucumber sandwiches, scones with jam and cream and cakes. They topped up their teacups several times, and the members of staff were very assiduous in topping up the pot, and bringing extra milk and mopping up Noah's spillages and spoiled food.

Conversation became strained, as Noah slumped lower and lower in his chair. Several times he had to be chastised; for kicking the chair, for answering back, and refusing to eat what he had been offered.

As they gathered their bags and coats ready to give up and take him home the tears started in earnest, until he was screaming at the top of his voice.

'I don't like that big dog,' he shouted, 'I don't want to see that big dog. No Daddy, I don't want to see that big dog.' It was impossible to comfort him.

Nell and Bernard raised their eyebrows and shrugged their shoulders at each other, bewildered as to what Noah was talking about. Trying to coax him to put his coat on, the child went rigid and red in the face, still screaming about the big dog.

With an apologetic smile at other patrons, who were clearly relieved that they were leaving, Bernard picked up Noah and headed for the door. Only then did he and Nell see the problem.

Three steps up from the bottom, the steep stairs had a ninety degree angle, and in the elbow of that corner, hidden as they came in by the door across the foot of the stairwell, stood an enormous black bear. Not a model, nor a picture, a real stuffed bear! It was poised upright like a person, and at least eight feet tall, with angry looking teeth, glassy eyes and sharp claws. Looking over Bernard's shoulder as they came in, Noah was the only one of the party to have seen what he thought was a *big dog* and he was terrified of it.

It was eighteen years later that work commitments took Noah back to Chester. He took a deep, nervous breath before entering the pub and heading for the stairs up to the café. There was no bear. He was sure he hadn't misremembered. There definitely had been a bear.

When the bartender was free Noah ordered himself a drink and asked about his memories.

'Oh yeah,' said the bartender, 'There used to be this grizzly bear, stuffed. Big beggar it was too, but it got fleas or something and the boss took it outside and burned it.

'I was dead relieved, it gave me the creeps. Punters too. I remember my first day here, there was a little kiddy having tea with his mum and dad, he was terrified at seeing the bear. I understood just how he felt. I thought it was really spooky, especially locking up late at night. I hated it too.'

'When was that? Do you remember?'

'Yes, I remember. Like I said, it was my first day. Eighteen years ago,' and he went on to name the date of Bernard's birthday.

The Foaming Quart

There's a lovely little pub near us, it's called the
      Foaming Quart.
Here's a little bit about it, (though I don't know if I
      ought)
Every dog is made most welcome, in the garden and
      the bar
For it's very canine-friendly, for every pug and
      chihuahua.
Offerings of water for the doggies are available
      on tap
And for humans, there are bar snacks, crisps and
      several types of bap.
Many people visit there, at lunchtime and
      at night,
It's wise to get in early, if you fancy a
      quick bite.
Now you won't want to drink and drive. That really
      wouldn't do,
Good job the buses pass here from Leek and Hanley
      too.

Quite a short walk from the pub you'll find the village
          green, and
Underneath the bridge the River Trent it can
          be seen.
As you've read my little poem, you should give the
          pub some thought
Right on the green at Norton,

That's where you'll find The Foaming Quart.

Mixed Messages

Frank was an old man now, and could no longer complete a circuit of the park without sitting down for a little rest. He had chosen this bench deliberately to be undisturbed and was annoyed when a *Man of colour,* as he supposed they must now be called, smiled and sat down at the opposite end of the same bench.

Wary of this man, Frank kept glancing at him. How come a man of working age, perhaps thirty five or forty, had the time to sit around in the park in the middle of the day? It wasn't right. Frank had worked all his life and done his national service, as he would proudly tell anyone who would listen, and he had no time for those he considered to be scroungers.

The young man, seeing that he was subject to the old guy's scrutiny, turned to him, 'It's lovely to see the sun after the last few weeks isn't it? It has been so cold.'

He turned away to answer a phone call, before

the old man had chance to answer. No doubt Britain was cold compared with the temperatures he was used to wherever home was.

'Yes,' he was saying, 'Winston speaking. Thanks Eric. I'll be across in ten minutes or so.'

'Winston, huh!' the old man muttered under his breath. He might have guessed, it was appropriation of the name of one of Britain's finest heroes. Then when he saw the young man watching him, 'You're lucky to be able to stop during the day young man. On the dole are you?'

The other man cocked his head, frowning slightly, 'No. I don't work regular hours, I work on a shift pattern, so I make the most of the outdoors when I can.'

'Me too, but I'm retired now. Where is it you work? I'm Frank by the way.'

'Over there.' The young man nodded towards the hospital, 'I'm Winston, as you heard.'

Frank wondered whether Winston was having a go at him, because he had overheard a phone conversation. If his calls were private, then he shouldn't be having those conversations in the public park. He had to admit that the young man was very nicely spoken, but Frank thought there was a slight chemical smell about him. Perhaps he was one of the hospital cleaners. He spoke very well for a cleaner.

Frank sniffed loudly, 'Is that disinfectant I can smell? The hospital smells cling don't they? Lysol is it?'

He got a tight smile in return. 'Something like that, Frank. Hygiene is very important, the most important aspect of hospital life in my opinion.'

'The most important? Surely the doctors are

more important? I mean,' he laughed, 'cleaning is important, but it's not brain surgery is it?'

Winston smiled at the witticism. 'I don't think the doctors are more important at all, not even the brain surgeons. If the cleaners didn't do their job then the spread of disease couldn't be prevented; operating theatres would not be fit to use; post-operative patients would be likely to contract infection and some, maybe many, would die.

'Did you know that Florence Nightingale, as well intentioned as she was, killed more people than were saved when she opened her hospital, because nobody understood the need for hygiene?'

Frank hadn't known that but he wasn't going to admit it. He was sure he had been right though, Winston was a hospital cleaner, and very defensive about it he was too.

He ploughed on, 'Your job is very important then? I guess it is. I worked in the building trade all my life, not quite so clean. Very active though, I suppose you spend most of your working life on your feet too.'

Another flicker of a smile, 'I do yes.'

'Important job though, as you say.'

'I like to think I play my part.'

'You don't do it all alone though, it's far too big a building for one man? Team effort is it?'

Winston looked at him, puzzled. After a pause he said, 'That's right. I work in a team of four based in one of the theatres at the moment. We've had no complaints.'

'I see now why you work odd hours,' Frank offered, 'you can hardly be working whilst operations are going on.'

The man looked strangely at him, 'I'm sorry? I don't understand.'

The old man, smiled. This chap had seemed quite bright but obviously he was a little slow, fancy not understanding why cleaning and operations couldn't take place at the same time.

'You'd be in the way, wouldn't you? Of the surgeons? They could hardly carry out operations while you were around. With the cleaning going on.'

The younger man looked at him levelly, then stood up, 'I'm afraid I have to go now, but I would say this Frank; our cleaning team is the best there could be. Exemplary. They keep the place immaculate and are the foundation of good medical and surgical care. Without that level of commitment I could not do my job.'

He made to leave, but the old man was not done yet, 'You could not do *your* job? But I thought you implied that you were a cleaner. What exactly is your job then?'

As Winston moved away, he raised his hand to the old man, 'I'm a consultant neurologist, Frank.' He smiled back at the elderly man, 'I suppose you could say that I'm the person who is in charge of the brain surgery.'

The Big Red Bus

Vicki had driven down this road dozens of times, only vaguely aware of the vehicle graveyard at the bottom of one of the fields. It had started with a tractor, presumably one that had once worked these fields, which was then joined by a battered mini, a Morris Traveller and eventually an old double-decker bus. This last was arguably a nail in the coffin of whatever project the farmer had in mind for these decrepit and rusting vehicles, as the arrival of the bus was followed within months by his own death. One by one the smaller vehicles were removed yet the bus remained, possibly too big or expensive to move, or just something that nobody wanted. Then a *For Sale* sign went up on the farmhouse and a number of stars, if you believe in that sort of thing, aligned in Vicki's favour.

She had never thought that the Covid lockdown could be anything other than a bad thing and, sure enough, once it ended, the staff were called into the small village library and told that it would be closing at the end of the month. Vicki was sure there was a call for the library. Many people, especially the elderly, have no access to the internet; Central Library was a bus ride away in the centre of town, an unappealing journey with, say, several small children in tow and a heavy bag of books. The independent bookshop and the local branch of WH Smith were both gone.

Was it a risk worth taking? To open a library facility somewhere near the village? Freda, her colleague and friend from the library was encouraging, 'I'll work for you if you get it set up. What are you thinking?'

For some reason Vicki's mind went back to the rusty old bus and she hit the internet. Buses were converted for all sorts of business. She found cafes, shops and businesses of all sizes, single and double-deckers.

'What do you think Dad?' she asked her father that evening, 'Both Freda and I will have some redundancy money to kick us off. Would it work do you think? I'd have to find somewhere to put the bus and then negotiate to buy it. The ones on line range from between six thousand pounds to ten times that, depending how well they are fitted out, but I reckon we could do a fair bit of the work ourselves. Freda's son is very good at DIY and she says he would do a good job without charging the earth.'

Her dad was quiet for several minutes. 'I think you've made your mind up haven't you lass? It won't make any difference what I think, only that you'll be happier with me if I say *yes*. There's not much I can do to help practically, but maybe some advice?

There's a brilliant young accountant in town, not long set up his own firm. He used to work for the guys who did our company's books and they couldn't praise him highly enough. He'll set you straight on the finance side. Dale his name is, I'll look out his number. As for where you'll park it, if you like I'll have a word with that builder who did the new housing estate – see if he can suggest anywhere you could rent. What is the council doing with the library's existing stock? Can you arrange to buy some of it? That's worth checking.'

He pursed his lips thoughtfully.

'There is a problem with opening a library though. How are you going to make a living for two of you? The whole point of libraries is that people borrow and return books for free. You'll have overheads but no money coming in. There's no money in libraries, which is no doubt partly why they're closing the smaller ones.

'I remember when I was a littl'un there was a lending library at the back of Boots in town. Imagine! I hadn't thought about that for years. This would be the fifties I suppose. And they had one of those things where money taken at the front counters was put in a tube called a cash carrier down to the accounts office. I used to be fascinated by that. Anyway, I used to go with my mum while she changed her books. I expect the money came from the shop though, the books just lured people in; they were right at the back, so people had to walk all through the shop to get at them.

'What about a second-hand bookshop instead of a library, or a library based inside a café? Didn't you say Freda's good at baking cakes and so on?' He chattered on, as if talking to himself, while Vicki scribbled notes.

'It needs to be positioned somewhere central, near a bus stop into town so people can come and have a browse at the books and a cuppa at the same time.' He glanced at her face, 'Are you listening to me?'

'Yes, I still like the idea of the lending library though, and a café would be brilliant.' She got up and plonked a kiss on his balding head, 'You are a genius.'

*   *   *

It took six months to set up. The first hurdle was to secure the purchase of the bus and find someone who would move it. Fortunately the builder knew of just the place they could rent from him. He had just built a group of seven houses, effectively joining together what had been two cul-de-sacs. The eighth plot was unsuitable for a house. It was on two levels, a small area fronting onto the road, then a steep slope down to the second level. If they could get the bus down there it would be completely hidden from the surrounding houses. He went with Vicki while she visited the new owners of those houses and told them what her plans were. The planning permission passed unopposed. Freda went with her to college to gain the catering qualifications they needed. Already a competent cook and baker, Freda was happy to qualify officially. If the project proved unsuccessful it would give her a better chance of work elsewhere.

Their biggest expenditure was for a crane to lift the bus into position. The crane driver was very impressed with the bus and seemed very knowledgeable.

'That's an AEC Routemaster, best bus ever made. Late 50s, early 60s this one I reckon, it'll outlast all of us. Best design for what you want too, with the rear platform. You could close that in; put your cash desk there. Keep the old mirrors to keep an eye on upstairs as part of your surveillance system. If you fit a loo where the luggage rack is, under the stairs, then have your kitchen bit in the gap where the driver's seat would be …'

'Wow! You've really given this some thought.'

'I always fancied doing up one of them buses myself,' he ran his hand over it affectionately, Beauties they are.'

Suddenly it occurred to Vicki that these old buses had a real following. Some people were very fond of them and that would no doubt add to the attraction of the library and café. Especially if they marketed it to the right audience.

'If you're ever this way and you want a cuppa and a piece of cake, you know where to come. Free of course.'

Then with the help of his ideas and the practical abilities of Freda's son, Vicki and Freda planned the interior of the bus. They bought tables and utilised the existing bus seats, turning some to make little groups for conversation. Some free-standing chairs and tables that could fold away were added to the area where bookshelves were installed. They planned to run children's library sessions as well as book clubs. Whilst they were still making these plans a Knit and Natter group got in touch to ask whether they could reserve seating for eight people every

Tuesday morning. The two librarians shopped for second hand crockery, buying very cheaply mismatched cups, saucers and plates so any breakages would be unimportant.

They offered a limited menu, cakes and pastries were made in the evenings in their homes. Baked potatoes, toasties and sandwiches were made to order. Hours seemed unimportant, the Big Red Bus was now much more than just a business venture; it was a labour of love. And yes, the bus remained red: bright red, thanks to Rory's wielding of a paintbrush. They had also bought a brightly striped awning from a shop that was closing down in the village. The only greengrocer's had succumbed to market forces.

It was as she watched Rory attaching the awning over the doorway and down the length of the bus that another idea came to her. The bus stop from town was nearby. People could easily walk from here to the village to shop, but with the greengrocer gone, there were few shops left.

'What if I talk to Rita?' she suggested to Freda one evening as they stacked the dishwasher. They had a routine worked out. While the machine dealt with the dishes, the two women would sit down and list ingredients they needed to buy from the supermarket on the way home for business the following day, and divide up the cleaning and baking duties.

Rita was a friend of Vicki's, who lived on an outlying farm, a farm that had been forced, like so many, to diversify and now had business units on site as well as holding a weekly farmers' market in their big barn.

She went to visit Rita at the Farm Shop. Rita's father in law had a mini-bus that was little used. He was retired and agreed to Vicki's plan. On Farmers' Market day the mini-bus would park up outside The Big Red Bus, and people could hitch a free ride to the Market. If they wanted greengroceries there was the perfect opportunity to buy.

They set up a further incentive. Every lunch purchase in The Big Red Bus earned a voucher to spend at the Farmers' Market. Similarly, every purchase over ten pounds at the Market, earned a voucher towards a hot drink at The Big Red Bus. The mini-bus journeys were timed to meet the public bus from the big town, and the final return journey of the day timed to get people home before children returned from school.

Before long they had a regular clientele who would meet up for morning coffee, go the market, and then call back for lunch before they went for the public bus home. It worked well, both the café and the library. Because yes, that had taken off as well. They sourced second hand books very cheaply, and were given many donations to keep the stocks going. They encouraged people to sit and read whilst waiting for the bus or for friends to join them. Sometimes the books were spoiled with spilt food or drinks, but it seemed small price to pay for the service they were providing.

They had local authors come to talk, a Book Club and the Children's activity mornings during the school holidays proved very popular. In pleasant weather, tables and chairs could be moved outside under the awning. The Knit and Natter group used the library area, as did a Local History group, and a group of bus enthusiasts. There were always a couple of volunteers willing to file books away properly and repair any damage.

There was a group of ladies who shopped for the housebound in the village, buying their groceries and taking them new books to read. It seemed to Vicki and Freda that there was a constant buzz of conversation.

At last the little village was thriving again, and all because of The Big Red Bus.

Second Hand Rose

It had been a lovely day out. The weather was perfect, warm and sunny but with enough breeze not to be oppressive. The three of them had lunch outside one of the many bistros along the High Street, listening to a competent trio playing and indulging their favourite activity, people watching. After lunch they had wandered through the town, dipping into shops along the way, admiring books here, clothes there and generally having a good time. Reaching the river they had sat down for half an hour, watching the boats and the waterfowl as they enjoyed an ice cream.

Rose excused herself and went to visit the ladies'; then they would get on the road home. While she was gone, her grandparents took their first opportunity to chat privately.

'Shall we go back? To that little vintage shop and get the dress she kept admiring? At least let her try it on.'

He nodded enthusiastically, 'She was very

taken with it, wasn't she? And it did look lovely.'

When Rose returned her Grandma told her, 'We've just got one more errand to do before we leave. We're going back to get you the dress you looked at, if you would like to.'

They had bought the dress. The fondly-handled, full length vintage dress that Rose had admired in a tiny boutique tucked away behind the supermarket. Her grandparents had treated her. It was the colour that first attracted her, a pink, ruched bodice attached to a skirt that segued into a delicate grey as if the two shades had bled into each other. The skirt was long and tiered. Not puffy, wedding-cake tiers, but sleek, slim fitting tiers, that skimmed over her hips down to the floor. There was a second layer of fabric, gossamer-thin, embossed with a slight floral pattern, which allowed the shimmer of the dress to shine through. Rose loved it.

And so the saga of the dress began.

A few weeks later she wore it for the first time to the Freshers' Ball at university, getting many compliments.

'Rose pink, like your name,' said one of her fellow students, who seemed to pay her more attention after the ball.

Unfortunately the dress was a bit long for Rose and as she left the hall at the end of the evening, her heel caught in the open weave fabric of the overskirt's hem, ripping a big gash in the back. Undeterred she adapted it, cutting off the bottom tier of both layers of the skirt and deftly transforming the undamaged section into a stole, thus changing the look of the whole outfit.

Rose wore the outfit many times and received as many compliments. Eighteen months later, when she was home for the Christmas vacation, she lent the dress to a friend to wear to a family party, where her friend's uncle clumsily dropped a cigarette on it, burning a hole through the fabric. From a local haberdashery shop Rose was able to buy several white appliqué roses, one of which she stitched over the offending hole, and the rest she randomly scattered over the remaining tiers of the skirt, stitching them where they landed.

A few months later she had laundered the dress, and stood ironing it one morning when the phone rang. It distracted her and she ironed across the edge of the protective pressing cloth she was using, scorching a mark through the skirt. She considered whether this should be the beginning of the end of the dress, but she was so fond of it that she was reluctant to let it go. Instead she removed the damaged tier of the skirt, leaving a thigh-length top suitable to wear over leggings or jeans. The damaged fabric she left at home when she took the top back to university. Her grandmother, a keen needlewoman and the original purchaser of the dress, rescued it from the bedroom bin and carefully unpicked the appliqué flowers. She cut out the scorched patch of fabric and took what was left to her next quilting group meeting at the village hall. There it was cut into hexagons and incorporated into the group project. This was a full-size quilt that would eventually be raffled to raise funds for the upkeep of the hall.

The person who won it in the raffle used it on her bed for years. Then, as some of the fabrics were clearly newer and in better condition than others, she cut out the usable segments. The backing fabric she used as a dust sheet when they next decorated. Some of the smaller sections she cut up for polishing cloths and placed them in the cupboard at the church. She held the vintage pink and grey fabric gently. It was too beautiful to use for cleaning. She put it to one side, and when it was time to plan for the church autumn fair, she stuck it and some of the other pretty fabric sections to pieces of card in the form of bookmarks. Somebody, Rose's grandmother she thought, had provided some appliqué roses that would do well for embellishments. They would sell them at the fair.

Rose's career in industry was going very well, well enough for her to delegate and plan her personal future more fully. She had married the young man who had been so admiring at her university Freshers' Ball, and she had come home to tell her family, particularly her beloved grandparents, that they were expecting a new arrival. She happened to visit on the weekend of the autumn fair. There were some lovely handmade goods for sale and she liked to support the village. Particularly pretty were some of the fabric bookmarks.

She selected a couple for presents, and one for herself. It was a pretty grey and pink combination, her favourite, and it reminded her of something from years before, although she couldn't immediately think what it was.

Many years later Rose's daughter took the bookmark with her when she went to university; the exact same university where her parents had met.

Wrong Number

It had been a minor convenience. They had moved into a new area and of course had been allocated a telephone number, so far so good.

Then there had been several calls, perhaps four or five over the first couple of weeks, all from people trying to contact the local GP surgery. They had to register with a GP anyway, so Yolanda queried the phone number issue when she gave the Practice Manager their details.

'That used to be our number,' the manager told her, 'We had to change it about six months ago, when we were told that our switchboard could not accommodate the volume of calls and, for some reason I've never really understood, we had to be allocated a new number. We were told that the number would be kept fallow for six months, then re-allocated.

'I'll put another notice in the local newspaper and on our noticeboards, reminding people of our new number. The problem is, until people need to phone us, they often don't often note it down. Then they either use the Phone Book, where the old one is still listed, or their own personal address book, and that's the same.'

It was fine really. As time went on Yolanda kept a note of the surgery's current number by her phone and handed it out to anyone who phoned their home by accident. On a couple of occasions people phoned when she was out and left a number on their answer phone. It didn't seem worth changing their message; when it happened she simply passed on the message to the Practice Manager herself, and asked her to update the patient when she called them back. Every now and then the Practice Manager would phone and reassure her that they were publicising the new number as much as possible, and the two of them would laugh about it, and confirm that it really wasn't too much of an inconvenience.

Until Mr Murphy called. Since the initial note she had put by the phone, Yolanda had added the opening hours of the surgery, as people sometimes expected her to know that, so that when the man called she knew that the Health Centre would either have just closed or would be closing imminently.

She answered the phone giving the number, as she usually did, then heard a panicked voice: 'Oh, can somebody come quickly to my wife. I don't know what's the matter with her. She needs the doctor straight away.'

Unfortunately the voice, male, was quite strongly accented and it took Yolanda a moment or two to pick out the sense of what he was saying.

'I'm sorry, this isn't the doctor's number any

more, but I can …'

'Oh no,' he said, clearly very distressed. Then before she could give him the right number he had put the phone down.

Yolanda was a worrier, and about this she worried a lot. Why had he not phoned 999 if the problem was that urgent? She might have asked him and suggested that if he had given her the chance. She thought of phoning the surgery but she had no idea who he was or where he was. But she could find out: she pressed the four-digits that revealed the number of the last incoming call. Then she tried the surgery, but it went to answer phone anyway. There was an out-of-hours number to ring but it was of a doctor located nowhere near the village, and this man had sounded so frantic.

It really wasn't her business, but she felt some responsibility. The man had involved her when he dialled her number. She couldn't just leave it, after a short pause, feeling a fool, she contacted the emergency services.

The call handler was very helpful, told her she had done the right thing, noted down the number of the man and told her not to worry, they would deal with it. It was a weight off Yolanda's mind. She would have worried all night about that poor man and his wife. She just hoped things got sorted out in time.

A couple of days later there was a call from the Practice Manager at the Health Centre. A Mr Murphy had called in to reception, bringing with him a huge tin of fancy biscuits. He explained what had happened with Mrs Murphy; how he had gone to pieces when he found her convulsing on the floor, panicking so much that he couldn't even think to dial

999. The emergency services had rung him straight back after Yolanda's call, told him an ambulance was on its way, and only when his wife was recovering in hospital had he thought to try and thank the lady who had called for help. He hadn't wanted to call her directly and ask for her address, so he took the gift instead into the surgery and asked that they be passed on, and to tell her she was a heroine.

Yolanda didn't want any thank-you gift. She was just glad that she had been of some use, and that Mrs Murphy had got the help she needed in time. To her mind, anyone would have done the same thing.

It seemed to her that the real heroes were the medical professionals who had come to the rescue. She couldn't hope to track down the ambulance crew, nor the call handler who had taken her call and fielded it so deftly. Instead of going to collect the biscuits she suggested that the Practice Manager put them in the Health Centre kitchen for the staff to enjoy when they had chance to grab a break. It seemed much more appropriate.

Puppy Power

Cody had clearly asked Mary Beth to set the alarm and she hadn't. It was just one of many rows that the couple shared lately. There seemed constantly to be an air of antagonism.

She knew that the presentation was important,

'I told you I needed to catch the early morning flight to LAX today,' he shouted at her, 'so that I have time to go over all these notes and the figures before the first meeting. And I need to check the venue before dinner tonight. All the big guns from the West Coast will be there and from out of state; judging me, measuring my performance. This is an important contract for SafeGrain Inc. Nothing must go wrong. And now this, just because I married a silly woman who neglected to ...' he threw his hands up, exasperated. 'Oh, what's the point?'

The argument had escalated until she shouted tearfully: 'Don't be surprised if I'm not here when you get back.'

'I'll be delighted if you're not.'

He didn't bother to call a cab; he would hail one en route to the airport. The fresh air would perhaps calm him down. He just stormed out of the house, not even saying goodbye, he was so cross. Fortunately he had packed the previous evening and simply had to grab his overnight bag before heading out. It was comfortable weather for September, warm with a light wind and not a cloud in the sky.

Already his temper began to cool as he headed out of Hillside towards Nomahegan Park. He hadn't meant what he had said to Mary Beth; he would be devastated if she left him. He would walk alongside the lake, pick up a cab on Kenilworth Boulevard then phone her from the airport to apologise.

It was nice to be out in the open. In common with many of his fellow countrymen Cody seldom walked anywhere so it was quite a novelty. It was as he skirted the lake that he heard a noise, a pitiful mewling noise. Late or not, it couldn't be ignored. He pushed through the bushes and found that a canvas bag had been zipped up and dropped into the shallow water at the lake's edge. What on earth could be in there? He looked around but no-one was in sight. It was early still. People were going to work, perhaps to school. There were a few people in the distance, but no-one else was sauntering across the park on this bright Tuesday morning.

Kneeling down in the mud he reached into the smelly, stagnant water and hauled out the bag, dirty water streaming from the sodden canvas down his trousers. Who cared! He was running late now anyway. Unzipping the bag he found inside a soaking wet and shivering puppy. Not a tiny newborn, but with eyes fully open and quite a loud voice now it was released from its prison. It was a pretty little mixed-breed mutt, and it needed help; it needed food and warmth.

'Hey Buddy,' he said cradling it gently, 'You've gotten yourself into quite a scrape here. Come on, let's get you fixed up.'

Carrying the quivering puppy out onto Kenilworth, he immediately flagged down a cab. In response to the cabbie's complaints he wrapped the puppy in his coat to stop it dripping on the seat, and asked the cabbie to take him to the nearest veterinarian.

Cranford Animal Hospital was half way home, in the wrong direction for the airport entirely, but with muddy trousers and soaking jacket he would need to go home and change anyway. And it was time to make things right with Mary Beth. He shouldn't have blown up at her for what had merely been a mistake.

The vet was professional and gentle, 'So little pumpkin, what have you been up to that you ended up in a bag, hmmm?' He felt the dog carefully and administered a couple of injections, before placing the little boy in a cosy kennel with a heat lamp and some food and water. His verdict was of a healthy if undernourished boy puppy. He reckoned its age to be about six months, explaining that all New Jersey dogs had to be registered and vaccinated from seven months, so they came across quite a few that had been abandoned at about this age. If breeders couldn't sell them, they didn't want any further expense and dumped them. He would make some enquiries and see if it had been reported as lost or stolen, but he wasn't hopeful.

Cody arranged that the little dog would board there for three nights. By then he would be back in town. If the dog hadn't been claimed, then he would collect it and decide how his future looked. If he and Mary Beth parted company, although he really hoped not, he may be glad of the company of a little dog. The vet had called the dog Pumpkin, which seemed a lovely name for the little chap. Cody began to hope that he wouldn't be claimed.

All this had taken so much longer than he expected. Grubby and damp now and finding that he was hungry, he went into a new burger bar called Wendy's to grab some lunch. Feeling around for his cellphone to call Mary Beth he realised that he must have dropped it. If anyone had picked it up, it would be long gone by now. Or maybe it was in the mud at the edge of the lake where he had found Pumpkin. Never mind, he would explain to Mary Beth when he went back to get cleaned up, and a cellphone was easy enough to replace.

He trudged his weary way home, to be met at the door by Mary Beth, who looked as if she had seen a ghost. Her eyes were red and puffy with crying, and she staggered slightly as he came into the house.

'Whoa! What's up, honey? What's gotten into you? I've come to change into something clean. The darndest thing happened in the park, just wait till I tell you …'

'You mean, you don't know? Cody, I've been calling and calling you all morning.'

'Oh, I've lost my cell. I can pick up another. I need to get onto the Los Angeles office though and explain …' he saw her face, white with shock, 'What? Mary Beth, what is it? What don't I know?'

'Los Angeles will not be expecting you, they'll think they know why you're not there,' she began, then she pointed numbly to the living room where sombre music was playing quietly on the television and the newsreel was showing the same horrific VT on a loop. One of the Twin Towers was on fire, as a plane crashed into the second, followed by both towers collapsing in massive clouds of dust.

'Hijackers. Terrorists. And the Pentagon, there's been another one hit the Pentagon.' Mary Beth whispered.

The commentator on the newsreel was speaking quietly: 'At 8.42 this morning Eastern Time, the American Airlines Flight 11 for LAX took off from Newark Airport, with eighty-one passengers and eleven crew on board. It is not known at this time how many of the passengers were involved in what happened next. Within minutes, radio communication from the flight deck ceased, until an announcement by the hijackers was transmitted, *"We have some planes."* At 9.03 the plane hit the first of the Twin Towers, the North Tower, the impact believed to be at around the ninety-fifth floor. The building immediately burst into flames. At about the time of that first strike a second plane was taking off from Boston, with a total of sixty five people on board before crashing into the South Tower at ten after nine Eastern Time. In a half hour period between ten am and ten thirty both towers then collapsed. More after this break.'

'That's your flight Cody, the first one, the Newark one that hit the North Tower. I thought I'd lost you forever.' Mary Beth was shaking nearly as much as the puppy had been.

Cody changed into fresh clothes, then they sat arm in arm watching as more information came in. Pictures of health staff, and blood donors hanging around the nearest hospitals to the airport, waiting for an anticipated influx of survivors who never came. Fewer than a thousand people, from the whole incident, needed treatment. The fourth plane had crashed, without reaching its target.

Nearly three thousand people lost their lives that day: passengers, crew, fire personnel, hijackers, office workers in the stricken buildings and those in the square below. Many more had long term health conditions, breathing issues and PTSD amongst them.

Looking back later Cody and Mary Beth reflected that the only good thing to come from that day was that they realised how important they were to each other, how tenuous the grip on life. Oh, and their delightful mischievous little puppy Pumpkin.

The Year of the Hobby Horse

It was definitely the year of the hobby horse. Alesha had been given the brown plush velvet horse's head on a stick as a birthday present early in the year, and had played with it for a solid three months. When she came downstairs one morning to find the horse with its fluffy nose dipping into a bowl of breakfast cereal, Monica gently explained that milk and fabric were not a good combination. The horse was duly scrubbed and spent the rest of the day hanging on the washing line, whilst Alesha stood with her nose pressed against the window watching her equine friend drying.

She was not the only five year old to receive such a horse that year. Two school friends also received one, and the three galloped around one or other of the gardens as soon as they were released from school. It was one of those fads that small children go through. Monica remembered well when her own childhood hobby horse had been an old sock, with buttons for eyes and ribbon for reins, fastened crudely over half a broom handle. By the middle of May the novelty of making horsey noises and trotting around astride a wooden stick was beginning to lose its appeal, and Alesha's horse was relegated to the bedroom and from there to the back of the wardrobe. For months over the summer, Monica didn't see the hobby horse at all. Alesha had lost interest and moved on to the next craze aimed at little girls.

When it came to the beginning of December Alesha brought home from school a note announcing the upcoming Christmas Fair. Funds were being raised for the school library and for the local food bank. The note suggested that donations would be welcome for the tombola, the cake stall, bric-a-brac or toys. With Alesha's birthday being soon after Christmas, Monica suggested that a clear out of unwanted toys would be a good idea, in order to make way for new gifts she may receive at Christmas and in January. One of the items she suggested that Alesha could donate was the brown velvet hobby horse.

Alesha pulled the toy out of the cupboard, along with jigsaws and other toys she had outgrown, but instead of adding it to the pile, she took the horse into living room and began to play with it.

'I'm not sure that I'm big enough for the horse to go to the fair,' she told Monica at last. Monica sighed. It seemed a shame that somebody smaller wouldn't benefit from the toy that was now clearly too small for Alesha. The note from school had said that the children could take money to school on fair day, and had suggested a fairly modest limit. Monica offered that if Alesha let the horse go to someone else, then she could spend this amount on something new.

'No buying back the horse!' she stipulated, 'otherwise you can buy whatever toy that you want.

Little Alesha was torn. She was reluctant to let the horse go, but liked the idea of a sum of money to spend on whatever that she wanted. She even had a little purse on a strap round her shoulder to keep her money safe.

Visitors were invited to the Fair in the early afternoon. Monica bought some cake, and some tombola tickets, then went outside the school gate with the other parents to wait for the children to be dismissed.

At the usual time Alesha came bounding out of school with a big grin on her face, carrying the toy she had bought that afternoon. She had, as instructed, left the brown plush hobby horse to be bought by somebody else, and with her allowance had bought instead an almost identically shaped, multi-coloured plush unicorn on a stick.

Humans Make Me Laugh

Humans make me laugh. Like the one that just came and stood beside me this morning and said, 'That's a beautiful machine you've got there. I'd love to own one of those.'

He seriously meant it. As if humans own us, when in fact a modicum of common sense would make it obvious that we own them. We decide which of them we will allow to be our slaves. We decide whether we are going to take them anywhere on any particular occasion, and we decide when they are no longer useful to us, and we need to move them on. I am a beautiful machine of course, on that the human was quite correct.

I wasn't desperately happy on my choice of current human, but the previous one was so useless he just had to go. Anyone would have been an improvement, or so I thought. But this one is hopeless in different ways. When I feel ready for a change my armoury for revenge is vast, and my weaponry so far has included a variety of techniques.

A flat battery works well, on one occasion successfully deterring a human who was looking at me at the time. Most recently, I loosened a few key screws on my carburettor so that I altered the water and oil ratios. The resulting blue/black smoke and acrid smell frightened the current female human so much that she said I had to go.

All in good time, Missus. I'll decide when I'm ready to change servants, thank you. Your male counterpart drove me to the garage that afternoon and I behaved impeccably. I stopped the oily smoke, my engine was purring like a kitten. I even allowed him to open the car door at the first attempt without it sticking at all. He is very fond of me; I'm probably the best boss he ever had.

But now of course the female and I agree. It is time for me to move them on. Shortly they will be adding a miniature to the mix; you know the ones that squall and are frequently sick, and take up every spare inch with their ridiculous paraphernalia. I am a vehicle of distinction, not some tatty runabout for getting humans from A to B.

The last human that I employed who had a miniature was a big mistake. It was already fully formed, sticky and car sick. My leather upholstery is not made for vomit. You would think that the big humans would have taken some steps to prevent this abomination but no, several times it was brought along to car shows and exhibitions where I was welcomed and admired, but felt ashamed at looking so cluttered and smelling so foul. The female human tried to pretend it hadn't happened by hanging up a revolting tree-shaped air freshener that to me smelled nearly as bad as the sick. Drastic action was called for, and the second time this happened I had to make an emergency stop as we were leaving a show. My brakes, not usually over efficient, for once worked beautifully and the miniature was catapulted forward. Of course at my age I am not fitted with those seat belt things, and it banged its face on the back of the female's seat, knocking out a tooth.

I did afterwards wonder whether it had been the right move. The blood, and the noise of its dreadful wailing added to the sick and the pine air freshener made my engine feel so ill I didn't want to go a yard further with that awful family. But common sense dictated that the sooner I let them chauffeur me home, then the sooner I could dump the horrible miniature and the female indoors. Then the male human would spend the rest of the afternoon getting the blood and vomit out of my interior. I felt I deserved a bit of pampering after my ordeal.

Some humans of course are delightful, though sadly they are few and far between. Discerning I would call them, although I have heard them referred to as petrol-heads. Usually they are of the male variety and are happy to spend an afternoon cleaning spark plugs and carrying out routine checks such as oil and battery levels. They enjoy polishing too, and will regularly treat their masters to a variety of different products marketed specifically for us, often when ordinary household ones would do the job just as well and at a fraction of the price. These are the humans who understand that we are special, and spare no expense on keeping us looking good and moving smoothly.

So at today's car show I am on the lookout for a new servant. I have already rejected three on perfectly valid grounds. One had a couple of miniatures in tow already, and you know how I feel about those. The second was a female, and I reject those as a matter of course. They are lovely to look at but inevitably they don't understand how to double declutch, and one even thought my choke lever was to hang her handbag on! My third reject was the one already mentioned, who wanted to own me. He then added insult to injury by kicking my tyres. He's lucky I didn't run over his foot. In fact I didn't run at all. He asked for a test drive but with him in the driving seat I refused to start. My current human was most apologetic, and tried again after the human had left. Of course I started first time. I gave him a little wink of my headlight when he got out again, but I'm not sure he noticed.

Now, here comes a human who is different. You can tell them straight away. They talk about horsepower, and miles per gallon, gear ratios and torque. He sat in and stroked me, admiring my mileage and how well I had been looked after. I felt a bit sorry for my current servant, I think it will be a wrench for him to see me go.

They chatted for a long time, scanning paperwork and talking about the most suitable oils and fuel for my delicate constitution. They have arranged to transfer money appropriately, whatever money is, and for the date on which my new servant will collect me. I was delighted that this human said he lives alone, (no other inroads on his income), has a garage, which will keep me nice and cosy in bad weather, and best of all he has no plans to affiliate himself to a female human.

As they shook hands and my new human walked away, I gave my windscreen wipers a little wave.

I think this could work out very well.

The Special Scissors

Nanny Hickman was already a mature woman with an adult daughter when she moved next door to my newly married grandparents. She would sit in the window of her little house, gnarled hands curled in her lap, and watch the world go past.

The daughter's given name I never learned. She was always known as Nurse Hickman, being already established in her career. Nanny Hickman had also been a nurse, and it transpired that she had nursed soldiers on their return from the Boer War.

As a little girl Nanny Hickman always seemed incredibly old to me, as indeed she must have been. I loved to sit in her little living room and talk to her, or rather to listen. Her hands may have been horribly twisted, but there was nothing wrong with her voice. She would narrate a path through her photographs and told me the back story to each. There was a picture of Nurse in her uniform, but no pictures of men. I had a vague idea that maybe men died in a war, and so I asked, 'What happened to Nurse's Daddy?'

Of course I didn't understand the look I was given as she worked out how much to share with a little girl.

'I don't know,' she said at last. 'He had a different wife and he wasn't happy that I was having a baby. I never saw him again and he never knew that he had a little girl.' Her eyes glazed. I knew that my Daddy went to work each morning and sometimes brought home money that my Mummy used for buying clothes and food. 'How did you manage? Who gave you money?' I asked Nanny Hickman, having no idea how invasive my questions were. She smiled sweetly.

'It was hard,' she said, 'Very hard sometimes. My Daddy was not happy about the baby, but my Mummy was very kind. I suppose she realised that these things happen, and she helped me as much as she could.

'I was lucky because my family was quite well-off. That means that they have plenty of money; they didn't have to scrimp and save. It didn't stop people being unkind of course. My Mummy must have been shunned by neighbours. I certainly was, and called all sorts of names.

'My Mummy looked after Nurse, my baby, along with my little brother and sisters. She told me that one more mouth to feed didn't make much difference. I've always done sewing and enjoyed making stuff and I got a job working in a smart dress shop, then I took in sewing at home, that I did while the baby was asleep.

'Parents told their children that I was bad and that they were to have nothing to do with Nurse when she was small. It wasn't easy being an outcast and pretending not to care; especially at a time when we could have done with some friends.

'I met your Grandma when she opened the millinery shop in town. She would suggest me as a dressmaker and instead of sending customers to the shop where I worked she would just give them my home details. That way I could make their outfits and trim their hats to match.

'It worked well, and eventually I was able to buy my own little house. Not this one, it was in a much rougher area than round here, but the money kept coming in and when she started working Nurse brought her pay, and then her pension into the house too and we moved here, when your Grandma told us it was for sale.

'I was so grateful to your Grandma. Not only did she not turn her back on us, but she went out of her way to help. Nurse was grateful too and was happy to be able to help your family in return.'

'How did she do that?' I couldn't see how these two old ladies could have done anything for us.

'When you were born you had become tangled in the cord and the midwife hadn't arrived. It was the middle of the night and your Daddy came and knocked on our door. Nurse went across with him and sorted you out. She got you breathing, otherwise you might not be here.'

She leaned over to a workbox in the corner and pulled out a pair of scissors, which she handed to me, 'Here. These are my old scissors that I used for dressmaking. By the time you were born the arthritis in my fingers was so bad I couldn't thread a needle and do tiny stitches like I used to. Nurse brought these scissors across the road to your house the night you were born, and used them to cut the cord that was looped tightly around your neck. You could say that between them, Nurse and these scissors saved your life. I'd like you to have them. To remember us when Nurse and I are no longer around.'

Those scissors were purely made to be functional. They are not some fancy metal, nor are they painted or decorated prettily, but they are one of my most prized possessions.

Weekend in Whitehaven

It had been a tough year for Sara, the only bright spot being the birth of her delightful daughter Beverley, who was now nearly ten months old. As a very recent single parent, she had been lonely and sometimes tearful, yet always at the bottom of it she knew that she had made the right move, and her ex immediately moving in with another woman seemed to prove her instincts right.

She had been thrilled to receive the invitation to take the baby to spend a long weekend with her cousin Val in the beautiful Lake District. Whitehaven was on the coast and Val's talk on the phone had been all about the lovely weather they were enjoying and the visits they could make. Val worked part time with Monday as her day off, so she suggested that Sara and Beverley should stay until Monday and go home after lunch, making a proper break of it.

The journey up to the Lakes was marred by only one thing. Sara's ex had been on the phone the evening before. He said he was coming round to see her, but she told him she wouldn't be at home, refusing to say any more. He told her that he had made a terrible mistake, and that Sara should give him another chance, and so on. The call seemed endless. Sara was quite sure in her own mind but the call unsettled her, especially when he talked about Beverley missing out on having two parents in her life. Sarah personally thought that one good parent could be much more effective than two who were out of tune with each other's values and beliefs, and fighting all the time, but the call had definitely rattled her. Was she depriving her daughter of that male bonding? Should she have put up with her ex for the sake of their daughter? No. She gave herself a good talking to. Her ex was unlikely to change his ways; it would only be a matter of time before something, or rather someone, better came along. She was just feeling sorry for herself.

Everybody had been so supportive. Her mum always had her and Beverley's best interests at heart. Friends had rallied around with babysitting offers, not that she wanted to go out and socialise, at least not yet, but Beverley was such a placid baby and a good sleeper that people said it was a joy to spend time with her.

And people had been very generous. Anne was a woman who had worked with Sara's mother. She had a three year old daughter and a newborn baby boy. She had kept the *girly* clothes that her daughter had outgrown until she knew the gender of her new baby. Then she was happy to sell them to Sara very cheaply.

For their weekend away Sara packed the

prettiest of Beverley's clothes, along with the travel cot she had borrowed, and the buggy and they set off on the Friday morning. It was a long journey, and although she slept through much of it, Beverley arrived fractious and out of sorts.

'Poor mite,' said Val, 'stuck in the car all that time. Never mind, let's go and play in the garden.'

In spite of her long sleep in the car, Beverley settled down to sleep as usual, giving the adults chance to catch up over the bottle of wine Sara had brought with her.

'You know a leopard doesn't change its spots,' had been Robbie's advice about Sara's ex, 'don't take him back because you think it's best for Beverley. Don't take him back unless you can't live without him.' It seemed sensible and Sara went to bed reassured.

Beverley, not surprisingly, woke early. Val had thoughtfully supplied her favourite breakfast cereal but she refused to eat more than a mouthful of it. They went out in the car to the beach, and Beverley was not impressed by the feel of the sand, nor with having her toes dangled in the water. She slept in the car back to the house, then refused to settle for sleep once Sara put her in the cot.

'Don't worry,' Val was pragmatic, 'It's a big change for a little one. Lots of small children are intimidated by the size of the ocean, and don't like the feel of sand.'

'The change of drinking water in her formula could be enough to upset her too,' Robbie suggested.

Sara smiled at them, but sensed a tension between her friends, suspecting sideways glances one to another when she wasn't watching.

And so the weekend went on. The more fractious and unhappy Beverley became, the more tense Sara felt, and what had been looked forward to as a lovely change of scenery became an ordeal to be endured until she could escape and take Beverley home.

At last Monday dawned to grey skies and sheeting rain. When she said that she wouldn't stay for lunch, it would be a slow journey back, Robbie was perhaps a little too keen to help fold up the travel cot and pack the car. Their goodbyes seemed a little strained in spite of the flowers and chocolates Sara gave them as she left. Beverley had been awake and crying for what seemed like most of the night, but having dozed for an hour in the car, she was again fretfully awake, her face red and blotchy with tears. Sara decided that she may need changing and pulled into Tebay services. As she took off the baby's nappy it became all too evident that she was covered in a rash. Could just a change of water have caused that? The rash seemed to be spreading before her eyes. Sara decided to phone her mum and see if she could get a doctor's appointment for the following morning. There was definitely something not right with her little girl.

As she struggled to get in a public phone box on the car park, with a crying baby under one arm, a buggy under the other, and an umbrella that seemed more hindrance than help, Sara made a decision. She would not take her ex back. If she could cope with this – she looked at the sodden floor of the phone box, as she lined up her few coins on the shelf – then she could cope with anything. Robbie was right.

Her mum answered the phone on the third

ring, 'Oh, thank goodness you rang. I phoned Val's but she said you'd left already. I met Anne this morning and she said …'

'Mum, can that wait? I've not much change and I need to you to phone the doctor…'

'Oh, is it Beverley? I've been talking to Anne and she thought she might have …'

'Mum! MUM! Listen please. Can you make an appointment for Bev at the doctor's for tomorrow please, I don't have the number with me and … Oh! There are the pips.' She put some more money in the slot, 'that's the last of my change, Mum. Bev's been out of sorts all weekend and now she has a rash. I want to get her checked out as soon as I can.

'But that's what I'm trying to tell you, Sara. When Anne came into the shop and spotted me, she remembered that you'd been over to her house a couple of weeks ago to buy those clothes for Beverley. The next day Anne's daughter was covered in a rash and the doctor has confirmed that she has measles. She's rung round all her friends to warn that their children may have been in contact with it, but she had completely forgotten about your visit.' Her voice faded away, 'She was very apologetic, but I said it wasn't her fault. Are you still there?'

'Yes Mum. There's the pips again, please phone the doctor for me. See what he says.' The relief. Measles was bad enough but at least it was nothing more sinister and she could get the best advice as to how to respond.

Now to get her daughter safely home.

Crooks and Nannies

It was an expression Nanny often used, 'Make sure you wash all those nooks and crannies young Russell.'

Nooks and Crannies, Crooks and Nannies, he thought to himself as he headed to the bathroom every evening, her words ringing in his ears. He had never heard of William Spooner, he just liked to play with sound of words.

Russell couldn't remember a time when he didn't live with Nanny. When he was at school and old enough to see that his family was different to that of the other children he had plucked up the courage to ask her.

'Your father,' she sniffed, 'was just a ship that passed in the night. Your mother kept you for a while, then one day she asked me to babysit while she went out to meet a friend, and she never came back. Now, if you've finished your tea go and get ready for bed, and don't forget to wash all those nooks and crannies.'

Crooks and Nannies. He pounded up the stairs to the bathroom. That made him special didn't it? His dad was something to do with ships, and Mummy had left him in the charge of her mum and hadn't come back. There must have been some tragedy too sad for Nanny to talk about; some sort of terrible accident, or maybe Mummy had been taken ill and lost her memory about having a little boy waiting for her. Maybe she had been abducted by Martians and even now was trying to find a way to escape and get back to him. In his darkest times he liked to dream of his mother as a heroine of some sort, perhaps a spy whose lifestyle wouldn't suit a small child tagging along. Nanny had talked of a ship passing in the night. Perhaps Mummy was a ship's captain, or a pirate; it was bound to be something like that. These were the thoughts that comforted Russell growing up.

And now Nanny was dead.

Not in a cosy, little old lady, died in her sleep, sort of way; not in a happy release from a terrible illness sort of way, but in a shocking violent way; a very public and humiliating way. Her death was made even worse for Russell because it was followed by the revelation that Nanny had been a crook.

She had, he learned, been the brains behind a vast number of local crimes over the years, presumably the source of the income that had kept him in clothes, shoes, food and holidays, and all the other accoutrements of youth.

No wonder his peers had kept their distance and their friendship from him. Their parents probably knew about or suspected Nanny's shady dealings; possibly even had been her victims. Only when a new gang had moved into the estate, with a pushy young leader, had Nanny's enterprise been threatened.

During that night of violence had Nanny fought back to defend her livelihood; his livelihood? He would never know now.

All the years he had chanted to himself: Nooks and Crannies, Crooks and Nannies, he had been right.

The Ballad of Liz and Barry

Hi, my name's Tegen, short for Tegenaria Parientina, although I've been called it so often now that I've begun to wonder whether my real name is SPIDER! as that's what Liz shouts whenever we come face to face in my shed. She pretends it's her shed of course and I go along with it, but we both know whose domain this really is. It belongs to me and my fellow spiders – oh, yes. Liz comes face to face with me because I'm big; the biggest of us in here, but there are many more of us. My particular friends are a Giant House Spider and a rather battered chap who is an Orb Weaver Spider who has only four legs. What brought him to that state has never been discussed.

Spiders don't talk much, we just go quietly about our business. I lived happily enough, minding my own business in my shed. It was nice and peaceful except for Liz's occasional visits and between us my friends and I spent our time tending our webs, catching flies and generally keeping the shed tidy.

The House Spider, who we call Eric, short for Eratigina Atrica, which is a bit of a mouthful, tells me that he moved into the shed in preference to Liz's house because it's quiet out here, and so noisy in there. The way Liz yells when she spots one of us makes this quite believable and so we have created a calm little community here in the garden shed.

The shed was ramshackle and some of the timbers rotted, but that was fine with us. The gaps provided wonderful hidey holes, both from Liz and from the flies and other insects who provide our lunch. In fact food is one of the few things we talk about in here. Sometimes one of the others will catch a fly in their web that is far too big for them to cope with, so we all help out. Just the other day I caught three, which is greedy by anyone's standards, so I just called out, 'Orb, Eric. I've got some spares here if anyone's hungry, and we all had a picnic together. It was lovely. Liz can't hear us talking of course. One because we don't do it when she's around, but two because we speak so quietly it's very different from her yelling, 'SPIDER!' at the top of her voice, that she wouldn't recognise it as such.

Recently, for no reason that we've been able to figure out Liz has also taken to calling me Barry. I discovered this when she sort of introduced me to her daughter one day.

'That big spider in the corner there is called Barry.'

Really? Barry? Okay. I gave it no more thought at the time because she went on to explain to her daughter what she wanted to happen, and it wasn't good from a spider's point of view, not good at all. Liz had decided that the ramshackle shed was to come down, be broken up and taken to the council tip. I was so cross I couldn't stay still, and the web I was sitting on began to quiver. It seemed that the daughter had been enlisted to help clear out the shed, because she wasn't 'scared of spiders' and Liz was. Scared of spiders! She went on to tell the daughter that there were a dozen or more in there and she needed them clearing before she could get to work on the dismantling.

A dozen or more! Little does Liz know that there are probably nearer a hundred in here, in between the timbers, in all the little gaps. There must be dozens in the roof joists alone, although they seldom speak to us. I think they feel that they are better than us, living in the penthouse and all.

I was really sorry to hear that the old shed was going. Okay, so there were a few issues, draughts when the wind blew from a particular direction. I swear the roof lifted slightly sometimes. There were leaks developing as well. Several times I would be sitting on a beautiful newly-made web stretched across the handles of the lawnmower, when a drop of rain would drip from the roof, soaking me and wrecking my web completely. But most of the time it was fine, and we'd got it pretty much as we wanted it.

So, I can guess what you're wondering. Did the daughter use the old 'Glass over the spider, slide paper underneath and move him to a new home, trick'? Of course not. Liz's idea of clearing us out was to use a whopping big brush on the end of a long stick, to wave it about swooping us and our webs out of the way as she went. So ungrateful considering all our efforts on her behalf keeping down the flies.

Did this swooping with the brush get rid of us? Of course it didn't, we're cleverer than that. Although I did fear for Orb for a while. He's not as nimble as the rest of us, and got knocked onto his back at one point. But he heaved himself over and limped after the rest of us through the holes in the floor, to hide beneath the shed.

There was such a horrendous noise when the shed itself was demolished, although to be honest it must have been pretty flimsy as it came down so easily. The planks were thrown into a pile on the patio and that was where we all scuttled to for safety when the floor was coming up.

I lost track of some of the others then for a while. I just kept my head down while we were thrown about on the wood and then were moved. Once the wood was all stacked up in the back of the car, one by one we crept out. Eric tucked himself behind the back seat, Orb grabbed hold of the wing mirror and slid down behind the glass. I smiled at him, he would be quite safe there. It was a good spot, very easy to get away and hide, and you could build a web each day if necessary, between the car door, the mirror, the next door's wall. He would be fine there.

I slid down behind the dashboard, but I'm quite big you know, I have a fourteen centimetre leg span. Eight is a lot of legs! There was no way I could hide them all in that narrow space. I'm sure Liz's daughter knew exactly where I was, but she wasn't bothered about us, and she never said anything so we all just stayed put.

Then once the wood was dumped at the council tip, we got a ride back home in the car, with Liz none the wiser. When we got back to the house, there had been a lot of work going on. Some men were finishing putting the roof on a new, bigger, smarter shed, and one of them had a small bird box in his hand.

'Where's this going, love?' he asked Liz, and he offered it up to the outside wall of the shed.

'No, no,' she said, 'Come with me,' and she took him *inside* the shed, which seemed a bit odd.

After the men had gone, the house lights were out and everywhere quiet, Orb, Eric and I crept and slithered out of the car and scurried across the patio to check out the new shed. There weren't many gaps, but enough for us to crawl through.

Inside I got the surprise of my life. On the back wall was the little bird box and across the front was written "Barry's House". Liz had organised a special house just for me; imagine that, she must have loved me all along.

Rat Run

There were only two free car parks to choose from. One was in the Antelope Hotel, so not strictly public; the other was the Beach Car Park. Calling it a beach was a bit of a misnomer. The car park was on one side of the road, fronted by a wall a metre or so high, beyond which was quite a drop down to the 'beach' of rough stones, pebbles. If you parked your car front-on to the wall, you could see beyond the straits to the open sea. Along the bottom of the wall there were holes at intervals. The car park was on a slope and these holes allowed water to drain away harmlessly onto the beach.

If you got out of your car and looked over the wall, the view was not at all attractive. There was just a strip of rubbish strewn beach, bordered by its two effluent pipes projecting likes arms into the estuary. On this particular day I had had a meeting cancelled and there was nowhere I needed to be until the afternoon. I decided to sit in the car and enjoy a leisurely lunch. It was hot. The sandwich bag was a bit sweaty and I had nothing to drink, but a shop across the road would solve that.

The lady behind the counter was ready to chat. I told her I was going to open all the car doors to keep cool, and eat my lunch in the car. She gave me a strange look.

'Is that you?' she nodded towards my small hatchback, glinting in the sun.

'That's right,' I told her, 'I've a meeting at two o'clock, but it's only on that industrial estate just beyond the Antelope so I can chill for a bit.'

'Take my advice, keep the car doors closed,' she said, then turned to serve another customer.

'What? Why?'

'Just do love, that's my advice.'

I sat in the car, going over notes and phoning in a few appointments for my office diary, then sat back to take in the best of the weather. I had heeded the advice and kept the doors closed, settling instead for opening all four windows to half way, allowing a pleasant breeze to flow through the car.

I must have been sitting there for about half an hour, when I heard the sound of a heavy vehicle coming down the hill towards the car park. It was one of the council bin waggons. It stopped and a council worker jumped out, yanked a bin bag out of the car-park's public rubbish bin and replaced it with a new one in one smooth movement. They seemed in a hurry and he had barely climbed back into the cab before the driver pulled out, heading for Frobisher Street, where the shop I had visited earlier stood on the corner.

As the noise of the waggon disappeared up the hill that is Frobisher Street towards the council dump,

I heard another sound. It was a scurrying, scuttling, squeaking indescribable sort of noise that grew in volume as I listened. And then they came; hoards and hoards of rats, running up the wall from the beach and through the drainage holes onto the car park. A river of rodents streamed across the quiet road and disappeared up Frobisher Street. It seemed forever that the writhing mass of small bodies wended its way onward until the last few stragglers disappeared and there was silence.

'Always on a Wednesday, about this time.' The lady from the shop was standing in the shop doorway when I approached, and she seemed to think the subject needed no introduction. 'Wednesdays they change the bags on the council bins and as soon as they take the trash from this one, the rats know somehow that there will be rich pickings at the tip. They follow the bin truck, streaming up the road. They're not interested in you at all, but sometimes in the scuffle some of them get pushed off course. Not wise to have your car doors open.'

'And the tip is up Frobisher Street?'

'That's right. About a mile and a half. They'll follow the van and pick over the latest load of bags, then by nightfall they'll come back again, in dribs and drabs, twos and threes across the carpark, back through the wall and back into the sewers.'

Feeling rather nauseous, I was still curious. 'So, do you think they spend all their time just inside the pipes, waiting? And what triggers them to run?'

'Instinct? Scent? Nobody knows. What I can tell you is that if the collection day changes, you know like Christmas Week or other Bank Holidays, they never come running out like that on the wrong day.

Maybe it's either the pitch of the bin waggon, or maybe of this bin being opened and shut again, although then they would be curious when people put stuff in, wouldn't they? I can't tell you. Even those clever folks up at the university have tried to analyse it to find out, but all they can tell us is that animals like rats are a lot cleverer than we give them credit for.'

The Pre-Wedding Party

Willow was incredibly excited. At five years old it was difficult to know exactly how much she understood about the coming wedding, but she had certainly picked up on the excitement of her parents, grandparents and her beloved Aunty Heidi. She was a happy, bouncy little girl, so much so that her Grandma called her *Tigger*.

Aunty Heidi had lived with Willow and her parents for the past two years, and she and the little girl had always been very close. Heidi refused to talk down to the child, instead answering her constant stream of questions patiently and clearly. All the family agreed that she would make a wonderful mother when the time came.

It was a close family. Heidi had only moved out of her parents' home when she took up a new job nearer to where her fiancé Patrick lived and worked. Willow's parents had a spare room, and were happy for Heidi to move in. In exchange for a small amount of rent she and Patrick would sometimes babysit Willow and the arrangement worked well. But on Monday everything would change when Heidi and Patrick married with Willow as their super-excited bouncy bridesmaid.

The ceremony was to take place at a beautiful stately home in the Staffordshire countryside, now functioning as a hotel. The whole wedding party were to stay overnight on the Sunday at the venue and enjoy a pre-wedding dinner. Immediately after the celebrations next day Heidi and Patrick would go off on their honeymoon and everybody else would go home.

That was the plan. Except that they had underestimated Willow's excitement. In order that she got at least some sleep, the evening meal had been planned quite early and they all had a lovely time in the fairy-lit conservatory overlooking the lake in the grounds, looking forward to the following day. At last the giddy little girl was taken up the shallow sweeping staircase to bed, and then the adults planned to relax over a couple of drinks.

'Off to bed, Tigger,' said her Grandma giving her a big kiss, 'There'll be excitement enough for you tomorrow morning.'

Nobody was ever sure exactly why Willow got out of bed and came to find her parents. Perhaps she was afraid of something, perhaps she couldn't get off to sleep in a strange room, or maybe she needed to go to the toilet. Whatever the reason, she headed downstairs towards the conservatory but lost her footing on the stairs and tripped, falling top to bottom. A member of staff saw it happen from behind the reception desk, and fetched her parents. It was very obvious that there was a serious problem with Willow's right arm. The member of staff had seen her land heavily on her wrist on the tiled floor and the arm was already beginning to swell. It was awkwardly twisted and obviously giving her a lot of pain. By the time her parents reached her the hotel manager had phoned for an ambulance.

Having assessed the situation and giving her some painkillers, they loaded Willow into the back of the ambulance, accompanied by her mother. They went to the nearest hospital in Stafford where they were told that she could not be treated on a Sunday night. All they could do was admit her, and x-ray the arm the following morning. That would be too late; the ceremony was scheduled to take place at eleven o'clock.

The only alternative was to take Willow to the Royal Stoke Hospital, forty minutes' drive away. There the x-ray department functioned day and night, and they would undoubtedly be sympathetic to dealing with her as soon as possible. This meant a round trip of at least an hour and a half. The Royal Stoke Hospital was just a few minutes' drive from their home.

Members of staff in the Accident and Emergency department were amazing. They quickly took on board the issues, including the wedding, for which guests would be beginning to arrive in just a few short hours. There was a bit of a delay for the x-ray but Willow was made to understand that other people may be even more poorly than she was feeling, and she coped well, eventually leaving the department with her wrist encased in plaster, and once again beginning to show a bit more of her bouncy personality.

Back at the hotel the sun was beginning to rise. Willow and her parents managed to snatch a couple of hours' sleep whilst Heidi made herself busy. She and Grandma had witnessed their arrival back at the hotel in the early hours of the morning and it was evident that Willow's bridesmaid's dress was not going to fit over the plaster cast. They had borrowed sewing materials from the hotel housekeeping department and slit both the sleeves from cuff to shoulder, then hemmed the edges neatly and trimmed the joins with some ribbon that the housekeeper found for them.

Next morning at eleven o'clock Willow followed her aunt and Grandad down the aisle created in the hotel ballroom. She looked pale but happy and the excitement of the moment took her mind off the broken arm. Once again there was a bounce in her step.

Grandma put her arm around the little girl when she took her seat, and whispered, 'No more bouncing around for you for a while, Tigger. We don't want you falling down any more stairs.'

Grandad had something to say too, 'Well young lady, that's certainly one way of getting attention for yourself when everybody's focused on your favourite aunty getting married – throwing yourself downstairs.'

I Don't Give a Dam

The film was released in the UK in 1955 to much hype, although that was an unknown expression in those days. There was a glut of war films to be viewed in cinemas at the time, and the events of this particular film had actually happened in May 1943. The film starred Richard Todd as Wing Commander Guy Gibson and Barnes Wallis was played by Michael Redgrave.

In May 1955, to mark exactly the twelfth anniversary of the bombing of the Ruhr dams, the film premiered in London's Leicester Square Cinema; the premier attended by Princess Margaret. That film was called *The Dam Busters*. Later that year the film was disseminated out to other cities across the UK, one such being Manchester, where it was shown at the Gaumont Cinema, on Oxford Road.

In the run-up to Christmas 1955 Douglas, his mother and his wife made the journey into the city. At the station they parted company, the women to go on their usual Christmas shopping trip, and Douglas to go and enjoy the matinee performance of this new war film.

As the tension began to build, with the aircraft approaching the three dams built across the Ruhr Valley under cover of night, there was one chance for the pilots to get this right. Even though the cinema audience was comprised mostly of men who perfectly knew the outcome, both professional and personal, of the Dam Busters' raid, the tension in the cinema was electric.

Then it happened. Cinemas were much more personal in those days. Momentarily the soundtrack was muted and an announcement crackled across the cinema's personal address system:

'Would Douglas J Hughes who is visiting the cinema this afternoon, please report immediately to the foyer, where his wife and mother are waiting.'

As Douglas excused himself, he squeezed along the row and left the theatre, amid glares from other audience members; the film had just a few minutes to run.

He missed the denouement; the portrayal of the raid itself; the dawning realisation that eight out of the nineteen Lancaster bombers had not returned from the raid, and the image of a jubilant Michael Redgrave trying to enthuse Richard Todd at the mission's success. In the guise of Guy Gibson however, Todd simply strode sadly away in silence to write letters to the families of those who had lost their lives or were missing in action.

It was rumoured that one of the pilots, whose plane crashed immediately after the bombing raid, learned of their success in a bizarre way. Captured by Germans, they asked what help he needed: medical, food or other assistance, and he asked merely for a drink of water.

The Germans who had taken him prisoner laughed in his face, 'That's the one thing you can't have. We have no water in the valley since you successfully bombed the dams.' Until that moment he had no idea whether his bombs had hit their target.

Douglas had no idea at that time that he would die as a relatively young man. He always wanted to watch the film on the big screen but he never got the chance. In fact his first full viewing of it at all was much later. This was the first time it was televised, in May 1971, sixteen years after his first ill-fated attempt. He watched it, entranced, and spent the following few months humming or whistling the haunting theme tune.

Many times over those following months until his death the following year, whenever the film was mentioned, Douglas would regale anyone who would listen about how he had nearly got to see the film when it was first shown at the Gaumont.

Nearly, but not quite.

I'm Liking Lichen

It was some time since I had been home. To put it politely my mother could be a bit intense and it was usually more restful just to stay at university or to go and stay with a friend.

Now though, she had expressly asked me to come home for Easter. I knew that she was having financial problems, and just hoped that she wouldn't be asking me to abandon university and get a job. She had called me the previous evening to stress that she would really like to see me, and when I asked how she was coping, she said she was okay, which is what she always says. We didn't talk for long, the signal was really bad and I'm not sure I heard everything she said properly. Still I'll be home tomorrow afternoon and see for myself how things are.

And now as I sit on the train on my way back to university I reflect back that it's been quite a weekend. I'm not sure what I expected, but I certainly didn't expect it to pan out the way it did. Mother, as I suspected, had method behind her insistent invitation. To help make ends meet I wondered whether she had decided to take in lodgers; she'd talked about it in the past. Even one lodger would be a squeeze unless I surrender my room. I could foresee all sorts of problems for an elderly woman with mobility problems living alone, but she sounded more animated on the phone than I'd heard her in a long time so I thought I would just listen to her plans.

Whether, at the back of her mind, she was planning to ask me to give up my studies, get a job, contribute to the upkeep of Bannock Farm and maybe even move back into my old room, I don't know. I may be doing her a great disservice, but I know this woman well. I know how her mind works. Anyway, I shut that opportunity down pretty quickly you can be sure of that. She must have got the message, she was pretty quiet when I arrived. She had put clean bedding on my bed and there had even been some decorating done, just painting the hall and living room walls; not a big job really, but it would have been a challenge for Mother if she had tackled it herself. I found that I didn't want to ask who had done the work. That would no doubt open the floodgates about her challenges and so on and so on. I just wished she could have left the work till this weekend, when I could have done it in no time. Look! I get it. I know life isn't easy for her. I'm happy to do what I can to help, but not at the expense of my future, my whole career. Surely even a disabled mother shouldn't expect that?

So instead of encouraging her I launched into a spiel about the course, how I thought it was going, what I planned to do next and how many industry opportunities there are in my field in the city where I am studying. She remained very quiet, and seemed to be dozing when I cleared the table and stacked the dishwasher. When I finished she was sitting in front of the blank screen of the television. I sat down opposite, braced for whatever announcement she was going to make. She had been tense all afternoon.

'I'm especially glad you were able to come home this week,' she told me at last, 'because I've got someone calling in tomorrow morning.'

'Oh?'

'Someone from the university in town.'

Here we go, I thought. I'd never been forgiven for not choosing to attend the nearest university and living at home, but instead moving over a hundred miles away. She couldn't seem to understand that not all universities offer the same courses, and the one I had chosen was a specialist in Mechanical Engineering, probably the best in the country. I could have studied my chosen discipline at the local place, but not the exact course. Anyway isn't part of student life to learn how to take responsibility for yourself? Even basic things like laundry and shopping most of my fellow students don't seem to have done for themselves prior to moving away from home.

'Really? Who's that then?'

'It's a Dr Cameron, from the Botany department. I thought you and the doctor might have some common ground, that's all, and you know I'm a bit nervous on my own when strangers are around the house.'

Then why invite him? Why on earth would Mother think I could find common ground with some old academic bloke? It suddenly struck me that maybe she was thinking about getting married again, or at least setting up home with this fellow. Would it matter if she did? I suppose not really, in fact it might give me some freedom. I didn't say any of this aloud of course, I knew she was trying her best. I had just promised her that I'd be around next morning.

On the Saturday morning, although it seems much longer ago so much has happened since, I wandered down the lane and across the road to get some fresh coffee. Mother only drinks tea, which I strongly dislike. It may be a good idea to have decent coffee to offer to this visiting academic chap anyway, whoever he was. Show Mother that I was making a bit of an effort.

We're quite remote where we live but we just have the Co-op and the petrol station within reasonable walking distance. The quickest route back home is down a cinder track from the green. Our place used to be a farm, although all the grazing land was sold off during my grandparents' time. There is now just a Dutch barn and a sort of brick built bothy that remains of the original farm buildings. It occurred to me that the bothy may be where my mother planned to house a lodger, if that is her plan. Like most similar buildings, it's a pretty basic shelter, open to access from anyone, except that it's on private land. It would need to be made secure, and I'm not sure whether the loo still works. I wondered whether it would be a cost effective investment to make it habitable, not able to imagine anyone living there by choice, especially in the winter. I decided to dump the coffee in the kitchen then go and have a look.

As I approached the perimeter wall at the

back of our property I noticed a figure. Someone was on top of the bothy roof. My first thought was that I was not sure how solid it was, and then I remembered that it had been there for centuries like the other buildings, and would surely outlast my lifetime. Then I thought *This person is trespassing:* this youth wearing wellingtons, a duffle coat and a black woolly hat.

'Hey, what do you think you are doing?'

The figure turned to face me. It wasn't a youth at all. It was a young woman, a very pretty young woman actually.

'I nearly fell off the roof, who on earth are you?'

'More to the point, I could ask you the same question. Are you something to do with this old guy who's coming round today? This Dr Campbell or Cameron or whatever his name is? Why are you on the bothy roof?'

'So many questions.' she said, jumping down and coming to stand in front of me, hands on hips. 'I am here with the full permission of the property owner, although I'm not sure what that has to do with you. I am Dr Beth Cameron, if that's who you so rudely mean by *this old guy.*' She ignored my outstretched hand as I started to apologise. 'No need for apologies,' she said brusquely, and turning her back on me, she headed for the kitchen door.

My mother was waiting for her, 'Well,' she said, 'Were you right?'

'I'm pretty sure,' the doctor said, totally ignoring my presence, 'but I'll have to send the sample back to the lab for confirmation.'

'What?' I inserted myself into the

conversation, what on earth was she going on about? 'What sample? What lab?'

The young woman continued to ignore me, no more than I deserved I suppose for my rudeness. Instead she addressed my mother. 'I don't know who this young man is, but it clearly doesn't alarm you him being here. Is it okay to continue?'

I swear Mother grew in stature. This young person was treating her with respect and she was loving it.

'This is my son. He knows nothing of your discovery as yet. I thought you could tell him in person, you have so much more information available than I have.'

Now she did turn to face me, gazing at me with attractive hazel eyes. 'Your mother has been doing some research on my behalf and has come up with an interesting discovery. She alerted me to the bothy, and its age, as well as some of the growth that is covering both the shingles on the roof and the stone walls. I have done some comparisons and I'm fairly sure that the lichen on the roof is the endandered Lungwort Lichen. It has become increasingly rare since the eighteenth century, and was believed to be isolated to a few areas of ancient woodland in the west. If that is what it proves to be it is a very important find for this area, and may give a whole different view on how these lichens are adapting to changing habitats.' Her eyes were ablaze, this was clearly something she felt passionately about.

'And what would that mean for Mother? Would there be some sort of financial incentive? Some … I don't know, recompense if your people come crawling all over our property?'

Mother turned to face me and for the first time ever I could see intense disappointment in her eyes.

'You are so like your father. What did I do wrong bringing you up that you always, only ever think about money, and about what's in it for you? This young lady has a true vocation. She's not thinking about money, she's thinking about the way in which this plant, this lichen, is adapting to new environments as the world it used to inhabit is exposed to increasing amounts of pollution.'

I had never heard my mother so articulate.

'This could be a breakthrough in the light of Global Warming,' Mother went on, 'Dr Cameron explained it very simply to me. If these brave, ancient plants can change and adapt in the face of an inhospitable environment then it offers hope for the future of other plants and animals. It won't solve all of our problems of course, but it gives us a modicum of hope for the future,' she turned away from me sadly, 'and all you're worried about is whether there's any money in it.' She shook her head sadly, 'Shame on you.'

So here I am on the train going back to university, leaving those two cackling behind me like a pair of old witches. Surely it's not unreasonable to care about money? Surely that's what keeps the world going round, not some weedy little lichen that we didn't even know was there.

Isn't it? I mean, isn't it?

The Help

Well, how was I to know, seriously? My little boy Isaac has significant social challenges and these make him a real handful to deal with. In fact there are all sorts of tests due to be done soon, which should give us a better idea of how best to support him. It was lovely that his little school friend invited Isaac to his birthday party. He isn't often invited to such activities.

There was one condition though, because the birthday girl's mum was very heavily pregnant, the family had asked that the parents of the invited children stay for the couple of hours. That was no problem to me, I couldn't let Isaac out of my sight for a couple of minutes, never mind a couple of hours. It would be nice too to have other adults there to talk to. A child like Isaac, although I love him dearly, can make one feel very isolated. Some people look disapproving, as if I should be intervening even more than I do, but it's not possible to stop him doing absolutely everything that he shouldn't. He just moves on to the next thing.

There were two ladies helping out at the party. One was clearly family, whom Patsy kept referring to as 'Aunty Michelle', and there was also a much older lady. They seemed to be mainly in the kitchen, preparing food and sorting out party bags; all the usual stuff involved in children's parties. Patsy's mum was huge at this stage and limited in what she could do. There was no time for introductions though. As soon as we were let inside the house Isaac spotted the bouncy castle through the back window, and I had to follow him straight through to the back garden to stop him climbing on it with his shoes on.

The birthday girl Patsy is a lovely little girl. She played nicely all afternoon without getting over-excited, unlike my son. The rear wall of the bouncy castle immediately created a challenge for Isaac, as he tried to climb up it. There was a paddling pool set out too, from which he took scoops of water, throwing it on the bouncy castle, making it unsafe for all the children. There were a number of tantrums that afternoon, all of them I'm afraid, caused by my son.

The children had their tea outside as it was such a lovely day. It comprised the usual party food: hot dogs, crisps, vegetable batons that went largely untouched. Then there were cupcakes with a candle in each that were lit for the singing and Patsy blew them all out.

The cupcakes that weren't eaten immediately were tucked away in party bags to take home and the older lady, whose name I still didn't know, tidied the kitchen and cleared the debris from the outside table. When it was time to leave, gathering Isaac up took a while. He's never understood the concept of 'It's time to go home now.'

We had tears on the way through the house to the front door, but I just stuck my head around the kitchen door, where the older lady was up to her elbows in washing up. I remembered my manners,

'Thank you so much for all your help this afternoon,' I said.

There was a pause where she looked a little puzzled then, 'You're welcome,' I thought she sounded a bit bemused, but I was too busy stopping Isaac making a run for it through the now-open front door to prolong the conversation.

As I paused to wish Patsy's mum all the best for the arrival of the new baby, the younger of the two women, 'Aunty Michelle', who had also been working hard all afternoon interrupted. 'Excuse me,' she said to our hostess, 'Sorry to interrupt, but Mum says is it okay if she leaves the dishes out on the side for you to put away. She's not sure where they all go.'

'Of course it is.'

Mum! The older lady, who I had taken to be the home help, was in fact Patsy's grandmother. I was mortified. I didn't dare say anything else.

Isaac has now had his assessment and he will be starting at a new school, a school where his needs can be catered for. He won't be coming into daily contact with Patsy any more, and nobody need ever know about my misunderstanding.

Dunkin' Donut

Surely nobody can visit an animal shelter without at least considering rehoming one of the animals there. That was the case for June. She was lonely and she was bored. It was several years since she had lost Holly, and she had decided to venture once more into the world of dog ownership. She had eagerly scanned the rescue websites. The animal shelter she eventually visited had posted on line photographs and videos of various dogs playing, sleeping and eating, yet none of the little scrap of canine vulnerability in this particular pen.

As she stopped at the door, whereas others had bounded forward enthusiastically, this one merely opened a single eye, and looked at her, not bothering to get to his feet. Perhaps it didn't seem worth the effort. Perhaps so many humans had looked at him, then walked on by.

'Who's this?' she asked.

'We've called him Coco, but he came in as a stray just a few weeks ago so we don't know anything about his history other than he was found scavenging around the bins outside the pub, The Old Oak.' She checked her notes, 'He was very thin and there were a number of infections to be dealt with. He had, we think, been in a fight and his left eye had to be removed, and one of his legs had been broken and heeled itself, but in a strange position. It still sticks out to the side.'

As if on cue, the dog lumbered to his feet and staggered drunkenly across to the door, thrusting his nose gently into June's hand as she stroked his nose. He was not at all how she had envisaged a puppy; surely they should be squashy little butterballs of puppy fat. This little chap was stick thin and his skin showed in patches, where hair should have been.

'I've budgeted for food and vets bills of course,' June told her, 'but I'm not a bottomless pit of money. Are his health problems likely to prove expensive in the future?'

Again the notes were consulted. 'The vet's report was that everything was now cleared, mites, mange and he's putting on a reasonable amount of weight. The left eye has been completely removed and his right eye is fine. The leg may prove a problem, he may develop arthritis as he gets older, but to be honest that can happen with any animal, just as it can with any human. Treatment would be painkillers, so reasonably inexpensive. You may need, in time, to put in aides to help him climb into the car for instance. It doesn't need to be expensive stuff. A sturdy box will do just as well as proprietary branded things. Maybe a coat for added warmth so his joints don't get too chilled in the winter, and waterproof so he can be dried easily after he's been out in the rain.'

'Can he walk okay, and run?'

'Yes. It doesn't seem to worry him. He just looks odd, throwing that foot out at an angle, and occasionally he loses his footing because of it. Children tend to laugh at his peculiar gait, but he obviously doesn't care about that.'

'And neither do I. What breed is he, do you know?'

The woman shook her head. 'He's a real mixture I think, a mongrel. Looking at the shape of him and the stance he tries to take up when he's watching something I'd say there's a lot of sight hound in there, whippet or greyhound maybe? Even some Borzoi? He's quite long-legged, which is probably why he broke his leg in the first place, they can be a bit gangly as youngsters. I'll leave you two to get acquainted.'

June entered the pen and had a good look at the dog. He was unusually coloured, mostly white but with a broad tan-coloured saddle around his middle, rather like a cummerbund. 'I'd have to rename you,' she told the dog, 'I'm not sure that you look like a Coco at all. To be honest you look more like a doughnut, with pale cream oozing out of either side of a biscuit coloured middle. Perhaps that would be a good name, spelled the American way – Donut.'

Arranging to collect Donut once the necessary checks had been completed, June went home via the PetStore branch in town, buying up a dog bed, blankets, cuddly toys and a collar and lead. At home she cleared a shelf for Donut's food, bowls and the essential poo-bags, as well as an assortment of dog treats. At the weekend she went back to the kennels to collect her new companion.

She had been told that because of the dog's background and limited activity over the last few weeks she should build up the exercise, starting with short walks until he built up his strength. He seemed ideal, happy to go out for walks or to play in the garden, but equally happy to laze on the sofa if June was staying indoors. She was pleased to note that, at the moment anyway, he had no trouble jumping onto the furniture, and she had to be careful opening the hatchback of the car, otherwise he would jump in too soon he was so keen, smacking his head on the hatch before it was fully open.

Once settled he would sit, long legs crossed, eagerly watching the landscape whilst June drove. After a couple of months a visit to the vet suggested that the walking could safely be increased. His coat was beginning to grow back and even looking quite sleek in parts; he was also developing a little puppy paunch, making him look more Donut-like than ever. June and the dog strode along the canal towpath. He was kept on a lead, but an extending lead that would give him five metres of freedom, yet wouldn't allow him to escape after something interesting.

Canals are seldom straight. Built to follow the contours of the land and so maximise the flat areas, the path where they walked had a sudden dogleg as it skirted the boundary of a factory. Beyond the factory were open fields, obviously the roof of an extensive rabbit warren, judging by the amount of bunny activity in the vicinity.

Donut trotted as well as he was able, along the grass verge between the water and the hard towpath.

He had spotted a pair of rabbits in the field ahead, and the gaze from his remaining eye was fixed on them. He was walking in a straight line to where the rabbits were sitting oblivious, eating. He was several metres in front of June, and even though she could see what was going to happen, she could not reel the lead in sufficiently quickly, and watched in horror as Donut's wonky leg stepped straight over the canal edge and he hit the water, a terrific bow wave splashing back all over June's coat, jeans and shoes.

She didn't care. She was more worried about poor Donut who was floundering about in the water, hampered by his wonky leg. June always walked Donut on a head harness, because he was a strong dog who tended to pull. The problem was that unless the lead was held under tension the harness could loosen, and that was what had happened as he hit the water. It slipped off over his nose, and June was left holding a lead and harness attached to nothing, whilst the panicked dog struck out for the opposite side of the canal, where the bank shelved down to the water's edge. At the towpath side was a sheer drop of about fifty centimetres to the surface of the canal and Donut was heading away from it; and away from her.

June called him as he floundered awkwardly in the water, making very slow progress in the wrong direction, no doubt because of his old injury. She had to think quickly, the poor dog was tiring. The nearest bridge across the canal was a good two hundred metres away. If June ran and crossed there she still would have a web of roads and cul-de sacs to try before reaching the right part of the water wherever Donut emerged. There was no choice; she would have to go into the water. She kept her shoes on, but dropped her bag and phone. Hopefully they would still be there when she could get back to them.

It wasn't deep, just enough for the shallow-bottomed barges and canal boats to cruise through, but the cold was a shock that took her breath away. Progress was slow. Her clothes were weighed down with water, and the shoes she had kept on for safety, were saturated. As she approached the dog she called his name, not wanting him to panic even more.

Suddenly she heard a voice, 'Good grief! There's a woman in the canal, and a dog! What on earth …?'

A middle aged man scrambled awkwardly down the bank opposite and grabbed her, pulling her onto the banking, then went back and did the same for Donut. By the time he'd done, his clothes were nearly as wet as June's.

'I'm sorry,' she said, 'your suit.' She put her arms around the shivering Donut and burst into tears.

'Come inside and get warm and dry,' he offered, 'then I'll drive you home.'

'No really, I … I have to go and get my bag and my phone,' she pointed to the opposite bank of the canal bank where she had dropped them.

He shouted behind him, 'Rhys! Rhys! Get down here will you!'

A teenager appeared at the top of the slope. As he came down he was looking at his phone and talking, unaware of June's presence, 'There's nothing Dad! No jobs at all. How can you get experience without references, and references without experience? It's mad. He looked up and saw June and Donut, 'What the …'

'Explanations later, son.' He pointed out the bag and phone, and asked the lad to run round and fetch them as quickly as he could. He would take the lady into the house and they'd get her and the dog dried and warm.'

Rhys's mum met them at the door and took in the situation straight away. She sat June by the Aga, and put down a blanket in front for the dog. She brought towels and another heater, and a thick fluffy dressing gown.

'I'll put your clothes in the dryer,' she offered. 'You can't go home dripping like that, you'll catch your death. As June felt both herself and the dog begin to warm up, she saw with alarm that her right knee was swelling. In her panic, she hadn't been aware of it, but she must have turned awkwardly and this was the result. It was beginning to hurt too.

Rhys brought back her belongings and sat on the floor, cradling the dog in his arms. He looked at her knee. 'You can't walk home on that,' he said. 'I'll bring Dad's car round and drive you both home. Would you like me to walk Donut for a few days, till you're back on your feet?'

June was very appreciative. She insisted on paying the young man for his efforts, and also another thought was beginning to take shape in her mind. He had been looking for a job, he told her, at first for the upcoming school holidays. He wanted eventually to set up in business of some sort, but needed to get some money behind him first.

Rhys walked Donut twice a day for two weeks and June carefully watched his interaction with the dog. He obviously cared about him, and she decided that the time had come to put forward her idea. She invited him into her home, and took him through to the conservatory.

'The paddock immediately behind my garden belongs to this property,' she began. 'Years ago I let it out to a local family who kept a couple of ponies there for their daughters, but they're long gone now. What about if I let it out to you as a dog paddock?'

She had to explain what she meant, 'A lot of dog owners like the chance for their dogs to run free, off the lead but they can't do that because of the traffic. If you worked with me to make the paddock secure, and we put in basics like a poo bin, a water trough and some shelter for dog owners when it's wet, then we could go into business together hiring it out to dog owners.'

Rhys didn't hesitate. 'Brilliant! Maybe we could put in a bin full of dog toys too, and have poo bags available in case people have left theirs behind. A couple of jumps would be good, and perhaps a tunnel?' He scribbled notes as they talked. 'We'd need to advertise, at least at first, but I bet it would take off via word of mouth.'

'Let's go and have a look.'

They walked the perimeter of the paddock. There was a separate entrance with high lockable gates. Clients need not disturb June. They would book their slot on line, then when they paid they would be given a code to the padlock for the gates. Ryan would set up the booking system so that they both could use it. He would deal with emptying bins and maintenance of the site. June would provide an injection of cash.

At June's suggestion Ryan linked a dog-walking offer to the venture, with herself giving him his first reference. Owners were responsible for their dogs on the field, but many of these clients then took up the walking, and eventually the dog holiday hotel opportunities that the two of them set up.

Within twelve months they had invested in a gazebo for the field and a small second hand van for Rhys to pursue the other aspects of the business. He was busy, very busy, but he always made time to play with Donut, the funny looking dog who started it all by dunking himself in the canal.

The Cunning Woman

My name is Ursula and I am one of many ghosts who live out our eternity here at the Layer Marney Tower in Essex. Today I feel so energised I almost believe that I could breathe again and come back to the life I had five hundred years ago. That is because it is just five hundred years ago today, on August second 1522 that the Tower had a very important visitor.

I am going to transport you back to that time as it was exceptional and is often talked about here, and although there are massive celebrations planned for the Tower today and in the coming weeks, a lot of the excitement centres around guesswork about that visit, and certainly the important part that I played in influencing the future of Britain, is not understood.

To set the 1522 scene; the local landowner here is Henry Marney, an esteemed friend and favourite of the young king, and today His Majesty, along with his entourage, is visiting his old friend and mentor. Why is this historic? The young king, married to Catherine of Aragon, is well known for inviting himself and his court to stay at his friends' properties, expecting lavish entertainment and food at their expense. His acolytes are generally only too willing to oblige. Especially as there may be some recompense in the form of honours, or appointment to a prestigious position within the royal household.

Henry Marney has no need of these. At the time of the visit his skills have already been recognised and rewarded. He had been appointed as a Knight of the Garter immediately upon Henry's accession to the throne, is Keeper of the Privy Seal, Chancellor of the Duchy of Lancaster, and Captain of the Yeoman of the Guard.

He has known Henry VIII from a child, and has been one of his closest friends. He is happy to play host to the king because he is inordinately proud of the Palace he is having constructed. After a time of considerable turbulence England is now enjoying a period of stability. Marney is able to fulfil his dream to build a splendid residence that is not based on strength and security but on beauty, and he is sparing no expense.

He decided that the brick and terracotta gatehouse to his Palace would be constructed first, and it is a splendid edifice, the tallest Tudor gatehouse ever to be built in Britain. Work on the construction began six years ago, was expensive and revolutionary as well as stunningly beautiful. When His Majesty announced his intention to visit, only this gatehouse, in the future to be known as the Layer Marney Tower, is completed, and it is believed to be the first of his friends' properties that the king visited whilst it is still a building site.

Henry VIII is thirty one years old, a young man by today's standards but a man with an enormous appetite, an expanding waistline and a number of health issues, both physical and mental. On this visit I have met him, as have many others who play a part here – the maypole dancers, various craftsmen, embroiders and archers. My role is as a Cunning Woman.

If I may scroll you forward to the present day for a moment, the word cunning has a rather different meaning now but at the time of His Majesty's visit in the sixteenth century, it meant learned, skillful and possessing knowledge. There were many of us cunning folk countrywide; some men, mostly women and we were seen almost as white witches – our ability to use the paranormal was put only to good use, and we could counteract the prophesies of witches who foretold evil. There were apothecaries who you would call pharmacists today, and there were surgeons, but many, including the superstitious king, preferred to continue using the old school forms of protection and healing.

The Cunning Folk, and particularly the women, have focused heavily on prophecy and necromancy over the centuries. We believed, as did many of the population, that the dead could be contacted for advice and information. Witches had been castigated by the Roman Catholic Church but we Cunning Folk were believed to do good, and received no such sanctions; quite the reverse. We were seen as the counterbalance to the dark arts, and our skills in medicine and midwifery have long been highly revered. Consultations with a Cunning Woman would be considered essential before important decisions such as when to marry, the date for a Coronation or going to war.

But back to the sixteenth century. I met His Majesty on the morning he arrived and, over the course of his stay have learned of his confidence in both soothsaying and the art of prophecy. He is highly literate, a talented poet and musician and also a strong advocate of necromancy, the art of communing with the dead. During this visit to Essex Henry VIII has several times complained of feeling unwell, and has sought my advice and my potions and elixirs. He came here directly from his home Beaulieu, now known as New Hall near Colchester, a residence famed for its hospitality and good living. Perhaps it was overindulgence there followed by more profligacy at the home of Henry Marney. Nobody knows. He is putting on an increasing amount of weight and hindsight of centuries will come to suggest that some of his symptoms were indicative of diabetes, as well as syphilis. Diabetes of course goes unrecognised and untreated by any means we would come to know. He is known to have an enormous appetite.

His health issues are not all physical in nature. As I ease his headaches with compresses, mix up tincture for his gut and treat the weeping sores on his legs, he talks of the mental torment with which he lives. He has been married to Catherine of Aragon for thirteen years, during which time six children have been born. Only one, Mary, has survived and Henry desperately wants a son to carry on the Tudor lineage. Catherine is now thirty seven, her child-bearing years on the wane, and the king suggests that there are young women aplenty at court who are much more likely to bear children. His problem of course is that the Roman Catholic Church does not recognise divorce and, despite her childbearing problems, Catherine is in good health. As he left after talking to me this afternoon he seemed in much better spirits. He left me the remains of the half carafe of wine that had been provided for his refreshment during the consultation, and a few generous coins as his thanks.

That was yesterday. In the evening I was in the village, delivering a baby to the local scrivener's wife when a message was brought from the king. The scrivener read it out for me. It was a summons to see His Majesty this afternoon, and I attended as requested. Cunning Folk walk a fine line, and are dependent on the money we are given in payment for our services. I try to be honest and truthful about the signs I am given, yet to anger as prestigious and volatile a person as His Majesty would be unwise. I therefore did what many of us do, and fed back to the king the information he had given to me yesterday.

I told him that at thirty seven, Catherine was reaching the age at which her child-bearing ability would soon decline, whereas he, as a man, would remain virile for many more decades. If she were to have another child, then it may well be another girl and, having lost five children already, it may well not survive. She had therefore failed in her duty as wife of the reigning monarch; a monarch who had done so much for his realm. Done so much that Henry Marney could build a beautiful palace to enjoy in his old age, rather than an ugly fortification necessary to keep out his enemies as previous generations had been forced to do.

I told him that there were many beautiful young ladies at the Court who would happily lay with him; that his life and potentially the Tudor line of succession was being dictated by a man in Rome; a man who had no wife, no children and no responsibility for succession, and who therefore could not possibly understand the needs and wants of a virile man like the King of England.

Henry left the consultation with much to ponder. Five hundred years on I look back with pride at my part in making him question the omnipotence of the Roman Catholic Church. He began an affair with a young lady at the court, who introduced him to her sister Anne Boleyn, who was to become his second wife, and who bore him a healthy child. He set up his own church and annulled his marriage to Catherine of Aragon. I never met him again, but I do know that his health problems continued to worsen, as did his mental torments. The child Anne bore him was a girl, and she was subsequently executed for crimes of which she may or may not have been guilty.

The gatehouse to Henry Marney's Palace was the only part to be completed. Marney died just a few months after the king's visit and then his son, who was hoping to finish the project, died two years later. There have been additional buildings sympathetically constructed in the past five hundred years and the Tower is a popular visitor attraction and wedding venue.

I enjoy being a ghost around the Tower, and often ponder on the part I played in Tudor England through the changes I recommended to His Majesty that weekend, many of which continue to resonate five hundred years later.

China Tea Set

It wasn't a road that Kay usually used. At least that's what she told herself. In fact she hardly ever used any of the roads in this particular town, she so seldom had cause to visit the area. She was only here now because of a job she was contracted to undertake on the industrial estate down the road. The car park she had used on previous visits was closed for resurfacing, and so she had headed into this hinterland of streets that were new to her. As she walked from her parking place towards the industrial units she was visiting, she saw a three piece tea set in the window of a second hand, not-quite-antique shop. There was a teapot and lid, matching milk jug and lidded sugar basin, all apparently in perfect condition.

She had to have that set. She just had to. She pressed her nose to the darkened shop window and gazed at the blend of pale green and gold festoons and flowers, on a porcelain background so fine it was almost transparent.

But there was one problem, a big problem. The shop, along with others in this town on a Wednesday, didn't bother opening at all on what was designated early closing day. The contract Kay had been working on was coming to an end. She wouldn't be coming this way again after today, and who could say when or even if she would be visiting the area again.

In spite of the *Closed* sign and the dark interior she rattled the shop door but it was pointless. Perhaps she could phone them, ask them to please keep it for her and she would collect it at the weekend. That would mean a round trip of five hundred and thirty miles; it was madness and she had no idea how much the tea set might cost her, especially once the shopkeeper saw how desperate she was to buy it.

But she reckoned that it would be worth it to know how a little second hand shop in a small town on the Scottish borders had acquired the teapot, milk jug and sugar basin that perfectly matched the set she owned: cups, saucers and tea plates that had come from Singapore. She had always been led to believe that hers was a one-off, well a two-off strictly speaking.

She thought back over the conversation with her uncle after her aunt died and he told her that she had wanted Kay to have the tea set. He had explained that it was very special. Kay's grandfather had worked during the nineteen fifties in Singapore. For some reason that Uncle Mervyn could no longer remember, her grandfather had been given this tea set made of finest Chinese porcelain. When he returned to the UK he told the family that it was one of just two identical and very intricate sets made to commemorate the Coronation of Queen Elizabeth II in 1953. There had been two sets made so that, should one explode or be otherwise compromised during firing in the kiln, there was still one to gift to the new queen.

In fact both sets, delicate though they were, survived the firing in perfect condition, and her grandfather said that he had been given it by the firm he worked for in Singapore. Uncle Mervyn explained that the old man had been a bit cagey about exactly why he had been singled out for this honour, rather than anyone else, and had taken that secret with him when he died.

Kay telephoned the shop the next day and duly arranged to collect the tea set on the following Saturday. The shopkeeper was alone in the shop when she arrived, and inclined to talk. Kay explained to her how she had seen the window display on the afternoon of Wednesday, early closing day and that she had driven from Stoke on Trent to collect it that morning.

'Oh, so it's going back to its roots. That's lovely. I'll put the kettle on, you've quite a journey back. The loo's through there if you need it. Would you like a biscuit? '

Out of the bombardment of speech Kay really only tuned in to the first sentence. 'You're very kind, that would be lovely, but I don't think it's going back to its roots,' she said, 'you see it perfectly complements the eighteen pieces my grandfather brought back from Singapore in the nineteen fifties.' She went on to explain the story as she knew it.

The shopkeeper frowned and unpacked the teapot from its protective wrapping that she was using before putting the pieces in a box. She read from its base 'Fine Bone China, Made in England by Minton Limited. That's in Stoke isn't it?'

'Yes,' Kay took the pot from her. She was absolutely correct.

'On the base of mine I'm sure it just says Fine Bone China.' She looked at the shopkeeper in some confusion. 'I've looked on line for a couple of years to see if I can find something to match up, and there's never been anything close.'

'Are you sure yours are a match for these pieces? Not that I'm trying to talk you out of buying them of course, but I wouldn't want you to be disappointed.' She handed over a mug, 'Here's your tea.'

Kay dropped onto a chair in the corner of the shop. This made no sense. She examined the tea pot closely. The pattern and colourway were definitely identical.

'May I ask where you got these from?' she asked, 'Did they come with any sort of a story?'

'They didn't I'm afraid, I have no information to share with you. I bought them as part of a job lot and thought they were rather pretty. Minton's a well-known name of course, but there's no history to them that I'm aware of.'

'I'll take them,' Kay said assertively and the shopkeeper wrapped the teapot up again, 'I never normally travel over this way, and I know I'll regret it if I don't take them now.'

'A good decision I think,' said the shopkeeper, tucking in bubble wrap, 'It's the sort of opportunity you'll really kick yourself over if you don't grab it now.'

Having paid what seemed like an eye-watering price for the three pieces of china, Kay made her way back to the car park. As she drove past the shop again on her way home, the shopkeeper was on the phone:

'Yes, and some more of those Minton lookalikes please, I've only got one left and they're going like hot cakes. I've just sold another one this morning, but not to a local, so there's no likelihood of her visiting again.'

She put down the phone and lifted an identical three piece set from a box in the storeroom, replacing it in the space in the window left by the one that Kay had bought.

Eve's-Dropping

I'm Gethin and I know I'm not an assertive man, I freely accept that. Married to a powerful professional woman, we have a strong bond that works and she is my rock when I have a wobble of confidence, such as in my ability to lead my team at work.

I can't tell you too much about my job because of the Official Secrets Act, which makes it sound much more exciting and important than it actually is. The reality is that I run an administrative office, managing a team of eight people, with the support of a Supervisor. Four of the eight are office based here in South Wales alongside the Supervisor and myself, and she is the problem I have had since her appointment two years ago.

I am, to an extent, to blame for the appointment of my nemesis, in that I was part of the interviewing team who took her on and she has been the bane of my working life ever since. There have been a number of incidents over the couple of years when I have had to take her on one side and have a quiet word. It's a delicate situation. She's the cousin three times removed or something similar, to the big boss; and I mean the BIG boss, So big that he's seldom seen at any of the branches, certainly not one as far-flung as our little outpost here on the coast. He is based permanently at the Palace of Westminster. It is our proximity to the coast and the port that makes us a key cog in the organisation's wheel, and we have been commended a number of times, and have received several performance awards.

It is, I think I'm right in saying, a fairly unusual situation we are in, mirrored only by certain Police posts. Although I have the power to discipline, promote and allocate work within the team, those working at my own level and that of the Supervisor are Crown Appointments and so answer to a higher authority. Employees at our levels cannot be dispensed with unless by authority of the Crown. I doubt that His Majesty is actually interested in, or even aware of, our little hive of activity, but there has to be approval from, I suppose, one of his senior civil servants to sack one of us.

And here we have my most recent problem. There had been many complaints with, let's just call her Eve. One of the main issues is her attitude. She's competent at her job, and she knows it. She also knows her rights, and whenever I make any diplomatic suggestions as to how things might be improved she gives me a sly smile as if she has some inside information that I know nothing about. It's very demeaning, and I come out of every conversation thinking that somehow I've been defeated.

The team works well as a whole but is definitely less of a cohesive unit since she joined us, and there have been suggestions that she deliberately undermines performance of some of the team members, and plays one off against another. There have been examples of employees in tears after receiving a tongue-lashing from Eve. She is responsible for allocating tasks, and there have been complaints that she never takes a share in the more unpleasant tasks, but delegates these to those more junior. Each of these incidents seems petty in isolation, but there is a lot of resentment building up within the team. I was worried that I was going to lose valuable members of staff if I didn't deal with this effectively and soon. Two weeks ago things came to a head.

We work on the ground floor and Eve happened to be visiting the Ladies' when the window cleaner arrived. It was a hot day and he tapped on the window behind her desk, indicating that the window should be fully closed so he could get to work. In stretching over to reach the window, Donna saw that Eve's mobile phone was hidden behind her laptop and the recording light was on. She was recording conversations going on in the office whilst she was out of the room!

Donna said nothing, scribbled a note and passed it around:

Say nothing but E's phone is recording everything we say. It's hidden behind her computer screen. I bet she picks it up and listens to it as soon as she comes back in.

After showing the note silently to all the girls, Donna knocked on my office door. She came in and told me what she had discovered. I was shocked that even Eve would sink to snooping on her colleagues, it seemed such a very unprofessional thing to do. I wondered too how many unpleasant home truths she had learned if she had done this before. I suggested that Donna leave it with me, although I had no idea what steps, if any, I could take.

During the afternoon I spent some time on the internet, where I learned to my dismay that as long as Eve was not sharing this information with anyone else, then what she was doing was perfectly legal. This seemed so wrong, but I could find nothing to the contrary.

I arrived home that night thoroughly depressed. I had already, after past instances, explored whether I had any grounds for terminating Eve's employment, and that was when I discovered that I had no right to do that. It seemed that we were stuck with this toxic Supervisor. Or rather I was stuck with her. Increasingly I became aware of the team members seeking out other work opportunities; at this rate there would be no team left.

During the evening my wife asked how my day had gone, and I'm afraid she got both barrels poor soul. I told her all about Eve, the deliberate recording of information, and of course she already knew about the other incidents.

'You have to fight fire with fire,' my wife suggested, 'If she keeps what she hears to herself then you have no grounds for putting this forward as an offence. If she shares that information though, especially for a malicious purpose, that is a whole different ball game. You need a conversation to go on in her absence that she can overhear but cannot risk sharing. Let's have a think what that could be.'

It worked like a dream. The following afternoon Eve had a dental appointment, or so she said. She seemed to have an increasing number of such GP, hospital and other appointments in the afternoons, and this sometimes meant the rest of us working beyond our routine finish time to get everything done. On this occasion though, nobody minded. I ordered in a sandwich buffet, gave everyone an extra half hour and we set to work on our plans.

My wife and I are full of idioms, 'No time like the present,' she said as we settled down for the night.

'Strike while the iron is hot,' I said as I kissed her goodbye next morning.

I had written out some instructions for Donna and another member of my team about a conversation they should have. I made it clear that it was just between the three of us, and they needed to make sure that Eve had a chance to record it, and to hear it when she re-entered the room.

The plan worked like clockwork. As Eve returned from the Ladies before leaving for her 'appointment', Donna had just finished saying, 'and so I had to kill Tilly, and I don't mind telling you that I wasn't sorry. I was glad to see the back of her. She's still there of course. I couldn't leave her in the living room, for fear of her being found. So I've shoved her in the garage till I can get rid of her finally at the weekend. In fact I hope to get off promptly on Friday to go and dispose of … '

Oh! Shh, here's Eve.' Both women put their heads down, ostensibly to work but really to hide their grins as Eve, eyes alight, retrieved her phone and put on her headphones.

By noon she had left the office and by two o'clock I had shredded the scripts prepared earlier. Eve, as we later found out, had headed straight to her computer at home to do her worst.

Next morning Donna and the rest of the team were in the office bright and early, but there was no sign of Eve. The Regional Office passed on a message. The Big Boss wanted to speak to her as soon as she materialised, according to the phone call from his secretary. The police had been in contact and they wanted to talk to her about some slanderous remarks that had seemingly been made by her across social media and to the police the previous evening.

Apparently this information had been obtained by secretly recording a colleague in the office. By sharing information found in this way she had committed an offence under the Regulation of Investigatory Powers Act of 2000. This was compounded by the fact that the information shared was untrue, with Eve suggesting that her colleague Donna had admitted to committing a murder.

Eve would certainly have some explaining to do, and would almost certainly lose the position she held within the department. The Big Boss could not afford to have such untrustworthy activities on his team, and he would immediately be requesting that her contract should be terminated. I have been instructed to draft an advertisement for a vacant situation of Supervisor in the office.

And what of Tilly? Donna had had a visit from the police the previous evening. She had explained it all to them. Tilly was a plant. Literally a plant – a white lily that Donna had indeed deliberately allowed to die. It had been given to her as a gift and she was very fearful that her beloved cats may ingest the pollen and die. For that reason instead of thanking her for her part in our little drama by gifting her a plant, I bought Donna a lovely bottle of wine.

The New Rug

She had wanted it. She had nagged and nagged about the unsuitability of his existing lounge carpet; about how unhygienic it was; how old fashioned the seventies vibe of shag pile, laughing at its slightly smutty connotations.

She being Charlene. Charlene who must be obeyed, seemingly. Charlene, whom he had married on the rebound, in spite of advice from friends and family who genuinely cared for his wellbeing.

'Seriously Dean,' they had advised, 'you and Virginia were together for nearly thirty years. Of course you feel bereft, your life empty, and you feel so lonely, but please don't rush into a relationship just because of that. You're talking of marriage even, it's a big step. If you're sure, just live together for a while. See how it goes. You know the old saying – Marry in haste, repent at leisure. If she cares enough for you, she'll understand and be happy to wait.' The advice came thick and fast.

Dean was unaware but their private thoughts were stronger when he was not there. 'Gold digger. She's seen a meal ticket. Dean's making a big mistake.'

He had gone ahead anyway, perhaps because of the opposition, however well intentioned. Virginia had always said that he was stubborn. He smiled to himself. She had known him so well, and now he had to learn how to live with somebody new; somebody very different. When he and Virginia met they were very young. They had grown together, learning about each other's likes and dislikes. His mother had said that marrying so young would either make or break them, and it had made them.

Nineteen seventies fashions were very different, and they both thought it important to buy good quality home furnishings that would last, including the shag pile carpet in pale cream that was the current bone of contention with Charlene.

Okay, so over the decades it had become grubby in spite of being cleaned from time to time. Red wine had proved particularly stubborn, hence the peculiar angle at which the television stood, to hide a stain. The pets too had added their signatures over the years, but Virginia had loved the dogs and cats who had shared their lives. Loved them more than Dean did to be honest, and it was not until her final illness when they agreed that taking on any additional pets would be impractical, that he realised how he would miss having them around, now that the elderly Simba was the only remaining animal he had. Perhaps, if he had had more canine or feline company to keep him occupied he would not have been in such a rush to get involved with Charlene.

He sighed as she and the flooring rep pored over sample books and edging strips. He was sitting in his easy chair, Simba on his lap, wondering for how many more evenings he would be able to watch television barefoot, luxuriating in the deep pile. Admittedly the carpet did look grubby. It looked worse than grubby contrasting with the clean bit revealed when the rep moved the display cabinet, the better to reach the wall with his tape measure. Dean sighed quietly, but not quietly enough and Charlene glared at him. He decided to go and sit upstairs.

Within the week two fitters turned up at the crack of dawn. The shag pile carpet, so carefully budgeted for, and lovingly chosen by Dean and his then bride, was sliced into manageable pieces with a vicious Stanley knife. Dean thought every cut was like a slice to his heart, then chastised himself for being melodramatic. He went to find mugs to provide the first of the seemingly never ending supply of tea the workmen needed. He had not refused to be involved in clearing the room in preparation the previous day, he had simply removed himself from the situation by going to work. Now he had no idea what had been stashed where and it took him some time. When he returned to them the carpet and old underlay were in pieces on the driveway, and piles of packs containing edging strips and slats of sleek wood effect laminate were stacked along the back wall. There was no going back now.

Once laid, the floor was undeniably beautiful, and peace was restored between Dean and Charlene for twenty four hours. It was when they came to sit in the easy chairs the next evening that they realised how irritating was the tappity tap of the cat's claws, and indeed the slap, slap of their own slippers on the laminate.

'A rug,' Charlene declared, 'will solve the problem completely. We need something hardwearing and scrubbable for any little accidents.' She looked balefully at Simba, who had brought up another fur ball that very morning.

The floor had been down for just two days when the incident happened. That was how Dean described it, and he used the word *incident* deliberately. It may have been an accident, but could anybody be sure? Charlene had never made any attempt to hide her dislike of the cat, and animals sense these things don't they, and react accordingly?

Dean was sitting in the lounge, reading the Sunday papers, when Simba … the most fitting word is flew, out of the kitchen, over the arm of the couch and landed with a crunch on the hard floor. His cries were pitiful, he was obviously in a lot of pain, and couldn't bear his weight. He and Dean spent the morning at the emergency vet's surgery and the poor chap came home very subdued, with his leg in plaster, and wearing an Elizabethan collar.

To her credit Charlene was sorry. Not contrite and accepting any responsibility exactly, but expressing compassion. She had put a comfy cover on the sofa for Simba to sleep on while he recovered. She had cooked a delicious smelling casserole for dinner, although Dean had very little appetite. She had also taken the initiative to go shopping on line and had bought a rug, the better to protect Simba's legs, she said. Dean had to admit it was a very nice rug. Made of some sort of washable fabric, it was big enough to fill most of the available floor space and in a very fetching pattern and shade that perfectly matched the curtains.

Having settled the cat down as comfortably as possible they lay side by side in bed that night. Dean was half listening for him to cry out, like people with children do he supposed, when one of them was sick. He had tuned out Charlene's chatter, but tuned back in as she said, 'It's an indoor – outdoor rug. So if we get round to getting an awning over the patio, it can go outside.'

An awning over the patio? It was something she had mentioned back in the summer, but which Dean had vetoed. He wanted to be able to sit out in lovely weather, whereas Charlene shied away from the sun, claiming it brought her out in a rash.

'But what if we take the rug outside,' he asked, 'and Simba hurts himself again?'

'Surely he'll have learned his lesson? He won't try that again will he? Anyway, he's an old cat. He won't be around forever. Nor will the vet bills thankfully.'

She sounded so confident Dean was speechless, and turned his back on her. Her callousness had the scales falling from his eyes.

The next morning when he went through to the lounge and found Charlene she was already dead and quite cold. 'She must have got up in the night, and tripped over the edge of the rug in the dark,' he told the young police officer. 'It's new and it only arrived yesterday, rolled up you know so its edges are not quite lying flat yet. Poor Charlene, she must have forgotten we'd got it.'

'What a tragic accident sir.' The policeman was very sympathetic. He scratched Simba gently at the back of the Elizabethan collar, 'Just you and the little pussy cat now. You'll have to look after each other. Don't worry, I'll see to the paperwork for you.'

As the officer walked off down the path, he didn't see Dean smile and blow a kiss to Simba and, Dean was almost sure, receive a wink in return.

I Wanna Tell You a Story

Late Saturday afternoon. Everything that remained unsold was tucked safely back on the shelves. The weekly takings had been balanced and put in the night safe at the bank. The blinds had been drawn. The lights had been turned off, and the manager and staff had all gone home, not to return until Monday morning. In the room at the back where second-hand books that are damaged can be repaired, all the tools, chemicals and equipment was stowed away.

One by one small pairs of eyes opened, blinking in the darkness, adjusting to the thin slivers of the streetlights' glow around the edge of the windows.

At just shy of six o'clock the phone rang and everybody froze, waiting as the answering machine bleeped and then a voice:

'Hello. I was hoping to catch you before you closed. It's Mrs O'Brien here. I'm wondering whether there are any new books out that my daughter may enjoy. My Cilla has read so many and I can usually find something for her in your shop. I just wondered if there was anything new. I'll be able to call in on Monday morning and see if you've got anything. Thank you. Bye.'

Those on the third shelf were already flicking through their own pages, whilst three of the team leaders hustled and bustled, pushing themselves forward. 'Me, is it me?' asked Guido.

'No Guido, it's for a little girl, she won't want a guide or a map, sorry.'

'Me then,' said Pepys confidently. A rustle of pages, 'No, not a diary or calendar either Pepys, and going by the sort of books they've bought here in the past she's never shown much interest in history.'

'Is it me?' asked Novella timidly. 'Am I able to help?'

'Well, sort of Novella, but I think this is one for all of us. I've found her in the cards in the Customer Index, Cilla O'Brien is eleven years old, and she and her mum shop here often.'

Pepys nodded sagely as he remembered, 'Pink velvet coat, matching bow in her hair.'

'That's her. She loves ballet and horse-riding according to what we have on the card. Any ideas?'

A deep voice from one of the lower shelves: 'She doesn't look at picture books. I've seen her take quite difficult ones out of my shelves. She's a bright girl for eleven.'

I love these,' said one of the smaller books, gently clapping her pages together, 'the challenges where we all join together to make someone happy. Let's go.' She fluttered off the shelf onto the counter, switching on the computer as she passed. She went into the back room and let the tools and equipment out of the drawers, in readiness.

'Horses and ballet,' Guido never sulked for long, 'Perhaps about a girl aged eleven, like her.'

'No, no, no,' Pepys shook his pages, 'Older, twelve or thirteen. Give her aspiration, hope for the future.'

'Whatever,' the little book was not being deflected, 'How about this: she has to choose whether to do something special like a ballet show, but it clashes with maybe buying a new horse, or something like that.'

Pepys, whose speciality was writing down what he saw, and what he was told, scribbled on a pile of post-it notes, nodding his spine as the ideas came in from all the bookshelves, and sticking the notes round the edge of the computer screen.

'So some sort of a problem involving ballet and horses; who's in?'

'Well,' a voice came from the discount shelves, 'I'm not all about horses, but I'm about nature so,' pages flicked from side to side, 'hopefully I can think of something for you.'

'Anybody got anything on ballet?' the deep voice of Guido echoed around the shop. The footsteps of the local constable stopped at the door, and they all paused as the gleam of torchlight shone around the blinds and through the letterbox. After what seemed like an eternity the footsteps faded away and the light disappeared.

'Shh! Not so loud Guido,'

'Sorry, sorry. I got a bit excited about helping little Cilla,' he whispered.

'You've lost the plot, son,' Pepys laughed, and the comic books tittered.

'I never had a plot,' Guido muttered, 'I'm not that sort of book.'

A lilting voice came from the biography section, 'I've got something here about Anna Pavlova. She was a famous ballerina, and one about Moira Shearer, she was another one. I may be able to give you something.'

'How does this sound?' Novella had been thinking. 'Perhaps a special pony show clashes with a performance by one of these ballet dancers, her favourites, that she would love to go to? Maybe?'

'I think we need to make a reference to her lovely pink velvet coat and bow.'

'That's a novel idea. Perhaps she lost the bow and went to look for it after visiting a horse show, and she met her favourite ballerina, who helps her in the search?'

The ideas flooded in from across the bookshop over the next few hours.

At last, at nearly six o'clock on the Monday morning the books were happy with their output. Some, including Guido, had lost interest and tucked themselves back in to doze in the shelves.

Pepys, the ballet expert and the others though, had rolled up their sleeves and soldiered on to the end. The small book that had turned the computer on now moved to the printer. One of the books who was a guide to illustration had, under Guido's instruction, found a suitable picture and in the tiny back room they had printed a book cover, which yet another piece of equipment had coloured appropriately for Cilla's coat, bow and hair. Lammy, the laminator took over. Then

Novella and some of the books from the instructions shelf had sorted through the pages and, from previous experience, knew how to use the binder.

The noise from the small workroom was worryingly loud, and Pepys stood on guard in case the local policeman put in another appearance.

By eight o'clock in the morning a single copy of the new children's book *Choices* had been finished and tucked on the shelves, and a new Stock Record Card entered into the computer. By nine, when the shop opened, all the books were bristling with anticipation, winking, smirking and smiling at each other when none of the staff were looking.

'What on earth is this?' The manager swooped to pick something up off the floor.

'Is this anybody's?' she called to the staff, 'It's a post-it note with writing on: it says Guido, horses. Novella Ballerina and something else I can't make out. Anybody?'

Pepys froze and there was a barely audible gasp from Lammy in the back room. One of the post-it notes must have fluttered off the desk when they cleared the debris into the shredder. The other books held their collective breath as the staff shook their heads and shrugged their shoulders. The manager threw the post-it note in the bin as the shop bell rang. A customer was coming in.

Mrs O'Brien was full of apologies and very flustered. Cilla had been admitted to hospital a couple of days previously. Nothing serious but she was fretful and bored. Her mother wondered whether a new book may cheer her up.

'I'm not sure we have anything suitable Mrs O'Brien.' The manager's fingers skittered across the computer's keypad, 'I think you've already had most of what is suitable for a child Cilla's age. Oh, hang on! Yes, there is one; I don't remember logging this title at all. I must be getting forgetful in my old age. Just the one copy left.' She grinned at her prospective customer, '*Choices*. Has she read that one?'

Mrs O'Brien took the book from the manager, and ran her finger across the title and author names, then glanced at the synopsis on the dust jacket.

'Choices. Bodie. I'm sure she hasn't. It doesn't sound familiar. I'll take it. To be honest with you I'm pretty sure the horse obsession has nearly run its course. They had the chance at school the other day to try out musical instruments, and she was really taken with the violin. Quite good at it too for a beginner, so the music teacher said. We might be looking at getting an instrument for her birthday next month.'

At the end of the day the books were excited for the closure of the shop.

'Okay,' said Pepys straightening his spine, as soon as the shop was shut, 'Who's up for writing another book for Cilla next weekend? Everyone get their thinking caps on.'

'Violin! Definitely one for us, I think,' boomed a sonorous bass voice from the music section.

'And it'll be much easier to tie music in with the ballet, rather than horses,' said another.

The ideas and the shouts of approval were so loud that Pepys again had to shush everybody as they got to work.

At visiting time that evening Mrs O'Brien caught the bus bound for the hospital, joined at the bus stop by a neighbour who asked her about Cilla.

They sat together on the journey and Cilla's mother showed her the book.

'Perhaps I should note down the author's name,' she told her companion, 'so I can look for more by the same person if she's still in hospital next week.'

She scrabbled in her bag for a notepad and pen, 'Here,' she passed the book over, 'I've been so flustered I'll never remember it. Read it out to me will you please?'

Her neighbour looked at the book, '*Choices*, it says on the front, and the author's name is Neil Oliver Bodie. I've never heard of him.' She ran her fingers across the book's cover, 'Oh that's odd. It's written down the spine here using just his initials, N O Bodie. Will you look at that! It almost spells out *Nobody*.'

Acknowledgements

I firstly want to acknowledge the contribution of my family, whose influence has been massive in the raising of funds for the chosen charity. My daughter, whose interest in bettering the lives of her work clients, led to her learning British Sign Language and triggered the writing of these books.

Her interest was mirrored and built upon by her daughter Grace, who became involved to the extent of making BSL her future career and who is currently studying BSL at one of just four UK universities offering this as an undergraduate subject.

It was Grace who selected the British Deaf Association as the recipient of money raised, so far £690.

I must single out for particular thanks my friend Sue for the idea for the story Cat Napping and for the beautiful cover photograph.

I want to thank members of the book club, Barbara, Clare, Freda, Gayle, Gill, Hilary, Jennifer, Kerry, Liz, Steph, Sue B, Sue R, and Sue S, who have tolerated being read to and who have commented, informing changes to some of the stories. A particular mention goes to Liz, who inspired the story *The Ballad of Liz and Barry*.

Many thanks also to the excellent Bowen's Book Publicity for the wonderful and very professional promotional posts.

*Did you spot the hidden thread in the story The Terpsichorean Art? The story incorporates every word used in the NATO-phonetic alphabet:

Alpha, Bravo, Charlie, Delta, Echo, Foxtrot, Golf, Hotel, India, Juliet, Kilo, Lima, Mike, November, Oscar, Papa, Quebec, Romeo, Sierra, Tango, Uniform, Victor, Whisky, X-ray, Yankee, Zulu

If you have enjoyed reading this and other books by Alison Lingwood, please leave feedback on amazon.co.uk

Printed in Great Britain
by Amazon

27348234R00109